REQUIEM FOR BUGSY

BY:

D.W. DRAKE

COPYRIGHT

Author's Photo by Jane Chouteau
jane@janechouteau.com
www.janechouteau.com

Book edited by Carol O'Donnell

Published by Savanat Press
http:// www.savanatpress.com
Published in the United States of America

ISBN: 978-1-7336163-7-9 Paperback Version
ISBN: 978-1-7336163-6-2 Kindle Version

TABLE OF CONTENTS

CHAPTER ONE

LOS ANGELES
JUNE 4, 1947
WEDNESDAY
2:15 P.M.

As I was driving eastbound on Wilshire just past La Brea, a fat cop on a motorcycle swung in behind me and activated the red light on the front fender of his machine. After steering my shiny new Oldsmobile to the curb and setting the hand brake, I watched in my side-view mirror as the grossly obese officer snapped down the kickstand of his motorcycle with the side of his boot and transferred his sunglasses from his face to his police cap above the brim. I was reminded of my longstanding opinion that the LAPD shouldn't let fat cops ride motorcycles. It was bad for the department's image. Every fat cop riding a motorcycle I had ever seen resembled a bumblebee trying to get to know a dragonfly in the biblical sense.

Captain Straight: "Now Matt, I realize that you aren't in the best mood right now, but don't antagonize this ridiculous looking fool right off. Maybe he just wants to give you a warning."

The Brat: "Bullshit. You don't have to kiss his ass. This is Los Angeles, not Leningrad."

The voices weren't coming from other people in the car because I was all alone. They were coming from inside my head. Three distinct voices had been jabbering away in there since I got too close to an exploding Japanese grenade on the island of Guadalcanal, which shattered my left leg and fractured my skull. The grenade blast must have screwed up the wiring of my brain or something. But I wasn't schizophrenic. (at least I clung to the notion that I wasn't.) The voices didn't represent separate distinct personalities, but just differing parts of my own. The first voice represented my logical, practical analytic mind. I called him Captain straight. The second voice spoke for my petty, selfish side. I named this one The Brat. Most of the smart-assed words that came tumbling out of my mouth came directly from his part of the brain and often bypassed my own. Captain Straight tried his best to intercept these wisecracks, but he was about as effective as a two-strand barbed wire fence was at keeping a pack of weasels away from a hen house. The third voice I heard in my head spoke for my libido, and I referred to him as Little Matt. He didn't often speak. Unless there was a good looking babe around, he wasn't interested.

Captain Straight: "Tell the officer a bullshit story that you were distracted by a bee flying in the window of your car. It sometimes works on cops, if they're really dumb or they're feeling charitable."

"The Brat: "Just tell Baby Huey here to hurry up and write the ticket. I'm hot and tired and I want us to go back to the office and drink some whiskey."

I cranked down my window as the cop waddled forward toward me. He had his ticket book in one hand and crumpled up a pair of thick gloves in the other. Wearing the standard blue wool police uniform shirt, he sported jodhpurs in the same shade of blue below his enormous waist and black riding boots. The jodhpur's side bumps, on his massive elephant-like legs, made him look even more ridiculous if that was possible. Around his massive gut was a black Sam Browne belt that could also have encircled Jumbo the Elephant and all his brothers and sisters put together with about a foot to spare. Hanging from the belt down over his crotch like a codpiece, was his gun in a flap holster. The cop's face didn't help his appearance either. His round head, small pig-like eyes, and multiple chins were sure to win him the prize as the ugliest, most ridiculous looking man in Los Angeles. I wondered if, under the police cap, his head came to a point too.

"Din Y'all see that thur yaller laht?" asked the cop.

"You'll have to go get an Arkie translator for that one pal," I replied.

"Whut?"

"I didn't understand a word you just said. Where you from? Little Rock? Pine Bluff?"

"Texarkana," said the cop getting red in the face.

At the end of the Second World War, for some unexplained reason that maybe an anthropologist might be able to explain, a significant portion of the population of hillbillies, hayseeds, yahoos and hicks in the State of Arkansas, together with their wives and gaggles of ragged children, all suddenly decamped and moved to Southern California. The migration must have looked like a scene from the movie "Grapes of Wrath," but with marginally newer vehicles, and unlike in the thirties, this time the caravans weren't turned back at the California border by the Highway Patrol. This mass exodus caused an acute shortage of hillbillies, hayseeds, yahoos, and hicks across huge swaths of Arkansas. The remaining women in that state, of sturdy southern stock, immediately began to pump out replacement hillbillies, hayseeds, yahoos and hicks as fast as they could breed them. I think these ladies' valiant efforts will ultimately prove to be for naught, however. As soon as these replacement hillbillies, hayseeds, yahoos, and hicks grow tall enough to peer over the counter of the local Greyhound bus station, they'll be out here in Los Angeles too.

"Y'all tryin to disrepec me?" asked the cop. I could tell he was angry now. "Gimme yer lahsense n' cahr registration."

My vehicle registration was in a little see-through folder held to the steering column of my car by spring clips. I unclipped it and handed it to the cop along with my driver's license from my wallet.

"Matt-hew Cole, it say har, is zat raht?" he asked.

"You can read too?" I said. "Why, I'm impressed. You know, I admire a man who can read as well as ride a motorcycle. Can you do both at the same time? Can you do any other tricks? Like, say, can you juggle four tennis balls in the air all at once? Can you scratch your nose with your big toe while whistling 'Moonlight Serenade'? Or, here's a harder one, do you know what the words 'carried forward interest' mean on your form 1040? Just write the damned ticket. My ass is getting sore sitting here."

The reason for my hostility toward the cop was that I was so pissed off that I couldn't see straight. I was a private detective by trade and when stopped by the fat cop, I was just driving back to my office after blowing a surveillance. For the better part of three days, I had followed a woman, the wife of a client who suspected her of being unfaithful, all over the city. I thought I was being cagy, staying three cars back from her car. When we were driving on Western Avenue she suddenly slammed on the brakes of her Buick convertible, got out and stormed up to the driver's door of my car.

"Tell Arnold," she screamed at me, with her hands on her hips, "that it won't do him any good to have some slimy baboon follow me around. Tell him I'll see him in court. Right now I'm going home and smash every one of his precious bottles of single malt Scotch whiskey in the liquor cabinet."

I kind of felt sorry for poor Arnold for about ten seconds, but then it came to me that he had brought it all on himself. I mean, he had to have voluntarily said "I do" at some point in the past, despite the fact that his bride must have looked like a youthful version of Ma Kettle.

After stuffing the traffic ticket in the glove compartment where it nestled with two or three others, I drove to my office building on Wilshire, near Hudson and parked in the parking stall that had a sign staked at the head announcing: "Reserved for Mr. Cole." I had a private parking stall because I owned a business in the building. Every year after the IRS and the California Franchise Tax Board finished their annual violent strongarm robbery of my person, and I paid all the expenses, the proceeds from A-1 DISCREET INVESTIGATIONS were mine.

Instead of going in the front door and taking the elevator up to my floor, I made my way around the back of the building intending to sneak up the back stairwell and enter my private office without being seen by Mrs. Adderley. That way I wouldn't have to tell her that I had blown a surveillance and she would have to assign another detective to the case.

§

At the end of the war, it took the government quite some time to return servicemen to the United States from far-flung battlefields, and separate them from the various service branches. As a result, most returning soldiers, sailors, Marines, and coastguardsmen didn't return to civilian life until early in 1946. After reuniting with loved ones, these veterans tried to pick up their lives where they left off before going off to war. After a while, more than a few of them began to suspect that while they were crawling through the mud in Salerno, Normandy, Saipan, or some other God-awful place, some 4F bastards back home were maybe crawling across the sheets of their wives' beds. Maybe the tipoff came in the form of a comment from the neighborhood snoop about a man's wife not being so lonely when he was away saving democracy, or discovering a matchbook from a nightclub in the bottom of one of his wife's old purses. Quite a few of these suspicious husbands hired detectives to find out the truth. That's where I came in.

I had started a one-man detective agency in 1943 when I came back from the island of Guadalcanal with a shattered leg that precluded me from resuming my prewar job as a detective for the Los Angeles Police Department. I eked out a precarious existence as a "peeper," which was a private detective who only did divorce work, until a few months after the Japanese surrender. Then I began to get busy. I had more clients than I could handle so I began to hire other detectives to work for me. I chose young, smart ex-army CID investigators just separated from the military and hungry for a job. Before long I had four detectives working for me and was so busy I didn't have time to keep up with all the paperwork related to my business. I just paid my guys at the end of every job and stuffed all the paperwork in a drawer, and when that was full, I started filling up another.

That all changed one day in March 1946, when Agent Charles of the IRS called me to the federal building for what I thought was going to be just a little chat to clear up some teeny-weenie misunderstandings. I was there for three hours and it was one the most unpleasant experience of my life, on a par with being blown up by the Japanese or being forced to watch a Fred Astaire movie. The Brat swore to me afterward that during that interview two burly IRS agents held me down and forcibly sodomized me with the blunt end of a pool cue at least twice. Again according to The Brat, they were trying to get me to spill the beans about some secret accounts I supposedly had in Switzerland. It was all ridiculous of course, I couldn't even spell Switzerland or even know where it was at exactly But I was pretty sure I could find it on a map, somewhere in the middle of Europe I thought. But I have to admit upfront that I have no independent memory of that part of the interrogation about the Swiss accounts. It's all a blank. In any case, I left the IRS office saturated with sweat and limp as Little Matt was at the time, I felt like Superman did that time Lex Luthor dusted his boxer shorts with kryptonite powder. I swore then and there that I would rather face a platoon of Japs hopped up on sake single-handedly than go through another government tax audit. I planned to fix it so that if I was summoned again, I would have a hireling go in my place and get sexually assaulted.

I put a help wanted ad for an office manager in the Los Angeles Times. The qualifications were quite simple. Each candidate was asked if they could straighten out my business records and make them decipherable to the IRS, and, in the event of an IRS raid, they were willing to hold off the feds with a Tommy gun long enough for me to escape. For the first few days, those that answered the ad were mainly desperate people looking for a job, any job. One applicant, a young woman, seemed to have the right experience but she was too attractive. Little Matt was doing cartwheels over her but I was afraid the little bastard would get me in trouble with the woman down the line. So I rejected her, prompting an hour-long shouting match in my head between Captain Straight and little Matt.

On the fourth day, Mrs. Caroline Adderley walked in my cramped little office on La Brea Avenue for an interview. She was about sixty, with gray hair, a somewhat pinched face, and wearing pince-nez glasses. She was dressed in a women's tweed business suit. Mrs. Adderley informed me that she had worked in the personnel department of the Buffums Department Store in Los Angeles for fifteen years and assured me she would be able to unsnarl my paperwork puzzle in no time. When she first walked into my office, Little Matt had taken one of his many strolls up to my brain and looked at Mrs. Adderley through my eyes. He just shook his one-eyed head and went back down to his rightful place and went back to sleep. I hired her on the spot.

Mrs. Adderley worked out fine for the first two months. She organized my files to the point that if I asked for a particular one, it was on my desk in two minutes flat. But then she started to push the envelope about her role in my office. Similar to the way Hitler acquired the Rhineland, Austria and the Sudetenland, Mrs. Adderley started to expand her role in my business. First, she took over scheduling duties and assigning cases to my detectives. When I called her on it, she replied: "But Mr. Cole, it will work out so much better this way, you'll see. It will free you up to do more important things." Right under my nose, she proceeded to hire two more detectives, a receptionist and an assistant for herself. The office was so crowded that it took me five minutes to wade through humanity to go take a pee in the washroom out in the hall. When I made the mistake of complaining to her about the crowding, she took it upon herself one day while I was over in San Pedro working on a case, to move the entire office over to bigger one in a new building on Wilshire Boulevard. I arrived back at my old office that evening and the place was empty and everything was gone, including all the furniture. I thought I was the victim of commercial burglary until I saw the note from Mrs. Adderley pinned to the wall giving the address and directions to my new office. I raced over to the address written on the note in a state of high dudgeon and confronted my office manager.

"You complained to me that the old office was too crowded. I just assumed you were telling me to find a more suitable space. Really, Mr. Cole, you have to be clearer in what you want when you state your wishes," she said while looking down her nose at me. Right then I knew I was licked.

"Mrs. Adderley, there's a presidential election next year. Until then if I happen to mention casually, off the cuff, just making conversation, just shooting the bull, that Harry Truman has to go, please don't hire someone to shoot down the presidential plane," I said in reply.

On the plus side, Caroline Adderley's management was playing off in my bottom line. Profits had improved to the point I could afford to move out of my rooming house and into my own apartment. I also bought a new car in which I was very proud. It was a 1947 Oldsmobile 98 Custom, two-toned, dark green on top and with a light green body. And it had the new Hydromantic automatic transmission. No more shifting gears for me.

CHAPTER TWO

LOS ANGELES
JUNE 4, 1947
WEDNESDAY
3: OO P.M.

I huffed and puffed my way up the rear stairwell. Stairs were hard for me to negotiate. My wounded left leg had permanent nerve damage and consequently, I suffered from almost constant, low grade but nagging pain, tingling, and weakness in the limb. I had to wear a metal brace like the kids afflicted with polio wore. On flat surfaces I did much better, getting around pretty good, but with a noticeable limp.

When I reached the third floor, where my detective agency was located, hot and sweaty and out of breath, I entered the long hallway that connected the stairwell with the elevators in the center of the building. About twenty-feet along this hallway was an unmarked door that was the back entrance to my private office. Congratulating myself for eluding Caroline Adderley, I fished out my keys from my right pants pocket, stuck the appropriate key in the lock and confidentially stepped forward. I was suddenly brought up short and banged my nose against the door when the damn key wouldn't turn. I tried again, twisting and turning for all I was worth but the key wouldn't turn. I was forced to limp down the hall muttering under my breath to the elevator landing, swearing under my breath, turn left, and go in the public entrance to A-1 DISCREET INVESTIGATIONS.

The place was laid out like most commercial offices of the time. To my left was a spacious waiting area containing several hard as rocks couches and chairs, all done up in the latest fashion colors. On the walls were framed prints of long-dead early eighteenth-century English horses. These pampered nags, who during their relatively short bucolic lives ate better than the peasants who took care of them, had no idea at the time that they would one day achieve immortality as decorations for twentieth-century business offices. To my front was a reception counter of polished wood, behind which sat our receptionist, Betty. She was a mousy, not very attractive brunette in her thirties who was as nervous and skittish as a yearling colt most of the time. Apparently, Mrs. Adderley didn't believe in hiring good looking women, because the lady she picked to be her assistant, Luann, looked like Betty's twin but with several thousand more hard miles on her odometer. This was probably a good thing, what with Little Matt being the lecherous little asshole he was.

When I walked in, Betty, who was wearing a headset attached to a long boom microphone for the PBX curving around the left side of her jaw, turned to me and smiled nervously.

"Good afternoon Mr. Cole," she said.

"My damn key won't work in the damn lock on my damn hallway door," I said, looking at her like a British judge looks at a defendant in the dock, just before he puts the black rag over his powdered wig and says, "I sentence you to be hanged by the neck until you are dead. God save the King."

"Yes, sir, we had the locks changed just this morning," Betty replied while trying to control her jerky head movements.

"Whose fucking bright idea was that?" I asked with not a little exasperation in my voice.

"It was my bright idea," said a voice behind me. I turned to look and there was Mrs. Caroline Adderley standing there with her assistant, Luann, behind her. Luann was so nervous she was rapidly hopping from foot to foot, giving the impression she was hovering about a foot off the ground.

"I have the perimeter locks changed every three months as a precaution. We store a lot of sensitive information on the premises. Here is the new key to your private entrance. And another thing, Mr. Cole, I wish you wouldn't use profanity in the office, it's extremely unprofessional," said Mrs. Adderley as she handed me a shiny new key. She was gazing at me with hooded eyes like a kindergarten teacher would stare at a particularly doltish five-year-old boy who had been caught playing with his wee-wee under his desk.

I grabbed the key from her hand, turned, and made a beeline for my office with Mrs. Adderley and Luann in hot pursuit. Apparently, she wasn't through with me.

My private office was spacious and sunlight flooded from large windows on the back wall. The desk and other furniture were modern, sleek and classy and all this shit was bought without telling me first. The first thing I did after walking inside my office was to remove my gun from its position in my waistband at the small of my back and lock it up in the bottom drawer of my desk. It wouldn't do for me to have a gun too readily accessible when Mrs. Adderley and I were having one of our little talks. It might lead to an unfortunate incident.

"Why are you back so soon? Did you confirm Mrs. Pine's infidelity?" asked my office manager.

"No, she made me over on Western Avenue. Came up to my car and flamed out at me. You'll have to reassign the case to another detective," I confessed.

"Mr. Cole! This will create havoc with my schedule. I wish you would reconsider my suggestion that you retire from fieldwork and remain in the office. There is other, less critical work you can do here."

"Oh, no, I do that and in no time at all my office will be in the broom closet and I'll be bringing you and Luann your afternoon tea and sweeping up twice a day. You can forget that."

"Well, never mind that for now. This might be a good time to go over our detectives' performance reports. LUANN!" she called to her assistant standing behind her. She never said Luann's name in a normal manner, but always hissed it like a stray cat greeting a snarling Doberman Pincer in a dark alley. Poor Luann jumped in fright up to about four feet in the air at this, and then floated back to earth with one eye twitching.

"Go get the folder with the performance reports from my desk," Mrs. Adderley snapped at the trembling woman who galloped off toward her boss's office like Seabiscuit on the backstretch at Hialeah.

I removed my suit jacket and draped it over the back of my office chair. Then I tossed my hat over onto the window ledge, loosened my tie and sat down.

The Brat: "Would you just get the damn bottle out? I need a drink real bad. While you're at it tell the Wicked Witch of the West here get on her broom and fly out of here."

I opened the middle drawer of my desk and retrieved a fifth of Jack Daniel's Old No.7 Whiskey and a not so clean glass and set them on the desktop.

REQUIEM FOR BUGSY | 21

"Mr. Cole, I wish you wouldn't consume liquor here. This is a professional office and your drinking sets a bad example for the staff and other detectives," said Mrs. Adderley. The reflection of light from the lenses of her glasses made her look a little like Heinrich Himmler. All that was missing was Heinrich's little copy-cat Hitler mustache to make my office manager a dead ringer for the SS chief.

I looked down longingly down at the bottom drawer of the desk containing my gun. In my mind's eye, I saw myself retrieving my Colt automatic pistol from the drawer and creating a smoking, .38 caliber third eye in Mrs. Adderley's forehead. Everyone has these harmless little secret thoughts and fantasies but usually tell no one else about them, except maybe their psychiatrists. But in my head, nothing was private.

Captain Straight: "Whoa there Matt. Control yourself. I don't think you'll like it in prison. Once the other inmates find out you're an ex-cop, you'd end up with an asshole big enough to not only use as a garage for your new Oldsmobile but plenty large enough to also store your fleet of motor scooters too."

I just sighed and splashed four fingers of the magic amber liquid into the glass and lit up a Camel cigarette with my Zippo lighter with the gold Marine Corps emblem riveted to it. In an effort to cut down on my drinking I had recently resolved that I wasn't going to carry around pint bottles of hooch and suck on their necks like a common drunk as I had in the past. Now I would only drink my bourbon from a glass. It made some kind of perverted sense in my crowded head that I wasn't really like one of those unfortunate guys down on skid-row if I only drank my booze from a glass. As I was taking my first sip, Luann flew in and made a perfect three-point landing carrying a manila folder, which she handed to Mrs. Adderley like Merlin presenting to King Arthur the magic map with the big "X" on it, marking the location of the secret cave containing the holy grail. My office manager started to sit down opposite me but I stopped her.

"Let's go over those reports some other time. I'm feeling a little peaked and want to be alone so I can figure out once and for all whether Einstein's theory of relativity really holds water or the crazy looking bastard is just putting us all on, " I said in a manner I thought was perfectly reasonable.

"Or?" asked Mrs. Adderley, getting snarky, "so you can sit in here and drink yourself into unconsciousness?"

"This," I said, while holding up my glass of whiskey, "isn't drinking, Mrs. Adderley. This is just wetting my whistle. Drinking is what I plan to do tonight. I've got a fifty-gallon oak barrel of Jack Daniel's whiskey custom piped into the water system of my apartment that delivers the perfect blend of bourbon and water every time. I aim to put quite a dent in it tonight. But rest assured, I'll drink every drop of it from a glass, except for the few gallons I'll use in my bath."

After an annoyed Mrs. Adderley and Luann left whispering to each other and closed the door, the voices in my head started chiming in with advice.

Captain Straight: " Why do you put up with that woman's insolence Matt. After all, she is your employee. You can fire her at any time and there would be nothing she could do about it."

The Brat: "Yeah but I'd think long and hard about that pool cue with the smelly handle stashed in the closet of the IRS office before you do anything too rash."

Leave it to The Brat to get right down to the nub of the matter.

I leaned back in my chair, put my feet up on the desk and took alternate long pulls on my cigarette and my glass of bourbon. As the familiar warmth from Jack's magic elixir spread outward from my stomach, the frustrations of the day started to fade and I began to think about my date that evening with my gorgeous girlfriend Billie.

I was interrupted by a loud buzz from the intercom on my desk. I swung my feet to the floor and sat up straight. I wasn't used to using the damn machine so I had to mash almost all the buttons on it before Betty's frantic voice sounded from the Bakelite box.

" MR. COLE! YOU'D BETTER GET OUT HERE RIGHT NOW!"

Quickly I retrieved my gun from the bottom drawer of my desk and racked back the slide to ensure there was a fresh .38 Super round up the spout. I then crept as quietly as I could out my office door to a position where I could peer around a corner at the reception area. My employees and I were in a business where we dealt daily with emotional, overwrought people who were capable of violence at any time. I fully expected to be confronted with an out of control husband who was facing divorce and financial ruin due to one of our investigations. Imagine my surprise when I saw that it wasn't a crazed husband bent on revenge and there to kill us all, but Carlo the mountain, all seven feet of him, standing in front of my skittish receptionist. Betty looked like she was either about to start screaming her head off or die right there in her seat.

I had last seen Carlo the mountain in 1944, about the time of the Normandy invasion, as I was leaving Micky Cohen's mobster headquarters after returning a shitload of stolen mob money. How I came into possession of the money, and the murders connected with it, is a story for another time. Carlo worked, or at least he did then, for the west coast gangster organization of Bugsy Siegel and Mickey Cohen as one of their muscle men and enforcers. He looked a lot bigger than I remembered him. Instead of being the size of a staff car full of Admirals as I remembered him, I could see that now he was as massive as a Southern Pacific locomotive. Then I realized why. With his cousin and boss in the organization, Tony Cardello, away in Las Vegas these past three years, there was no one to regulate the mountain's intake of pasta. Carlo was dressed in a big gray felt hat and an expensive suit with enough cloth in it to make up all the uniforms for the musician's in the Chinese-American Drum and Bugle Corps, with the baton twirler's panties thrown in to boot. I decided I would have to quit calling him Carlo the mountain. From now on, he would be Carlo the mountain and a half.

I put my gun away and walked around the corner into Carlo's sight. He looked at me and his gigantic, very Italian looking face broke into a big smile.

"Hey Peeper, long time no see," he said and looked around the reception area. "Kinda looks like you're doin' alright for yourself."

"Just an illusion Carlo, if all the people I owe money to ever start talking to each other, I'll be like a crippled Harry Truman surrounded by a pack of hungry Republicans," I replied.

"Peeper, I need to tell you somethin. Is there someplace private where we can talk?

"Yeah, follow me but walk down the center of the hallway, I don't want you to brush the paintings off the walls. That shit costs money and it's not paid for yet."

I led him to my office where we sat down facing each other across my desk. Well, I sat. Carlo didn't fit in the chair, so he kind of perched on the front edge of the seat. I thought I could hear the sturdy oak frame of the chair crying out in pain, but maybe I imagined it.

"Tony sent me here to tell you that he needs to see you. There's something he wants you to do."

I didn't answer right away. The last thing I wanted to do was get mixed up with gangsters again, particularly these gangsters. The last time had been quite enough thank you.

Captain Straight: "Tell him you have to testify in court all this week and the judge will put you in jail if you don't show up."

The Brat: "Tell him a falling safe just mashed your grandma into a red mist and you have to go to the funeral."

Captain Straight: "Tell him you have an incurable disease and you expect to be dead and in the ground by next Tuesday."

The Brat: "Tell him President Truman thinks Bess is cheating on him and he's hired you to follow the lying, unfaithful bitch around Washington D.C. and film her secret trysts with that senator from Iowa."

"Is Tony Cardello back in town?" I asked. "Sure, I'll meet with Tony and hear what he has to say."

"Tony is still in Las Vegas. He wants you to come there," said Carlo.

"Las Vegas? That's 270 miles away. I can't go all of the way to Las Vegas unless I know what this is about," I replied.

Carlo looked at me strangely. It was like he didn't comprehend what I was saying. Then I realized why he was baffled. In his line of work, he told people to do or not to do things and they promptly obeyed or regretted it later. Niceties, like not inconveniencing people, or putting folks to a lot of unnecessary trouble, were not within his comprehension. Tony had told Carlo to come to get me and bring me to Las Vegas and that was that. Ordinarily, when confronted by people with outrageous demands I just say no or make a joke about it. But Carlo was another story because he had the ability to reach out with a hand as big as South Bend, Indiana and pop my head like a grape between two gnarled fingers. I shrugged my shoulders. It looked like I was going to Las Vegas.

"When does he want me to come to Las Vegas?"

Carlo gave me another strange look. "How about now?" he said.

"Carlo, give me a break. I can't go until tomorrow morning. I've got a date with my girlfriend tonight. She told me if I stand her up one more time, she won't go out with me anymore. How about we meet here tomorrow at seven?"

"Seven in the morning?" asked Carlo then rumbled with laughter. "Hell, even the pigeons are still asleep at seven in the morning."

We finally settled on 10:30 A.M. I made a mental note to write a letter of advice to the FBI. If they only knew that if they raided these gangsters before nine in the morning, they could catch them while they are all still in their pajamas, fast asleep, and with their Tommy guns unloaded.

CHAPTER THREE

US ROUTE 91, 60 MILES NORTHEAST OF BARSTOW
JUNE 5, 1947
THURSDAY
3:20 P.M.

GOLDEN NUGGET CASINO!, NICKLE SLOT MACHINES! Read the billboard as my car whizzed past. The view forward out of my windshield showed a barren landscape of desperate desert bushes struggling to survive amid miles and miles of big rocks, little rocks, and sand. Mountains were visible in the distance to my right and left, but these weren't the scenic kind. They were sun-baked, wind scarred and ugly humps of rock resembling ancient piles of dinosaur droppings. The only sign of civilization was the black ribbon of road stretching out straight as an arrow in front of me to infinity, and the occasional roadside sign.

I was scrunched up against the driver's door of my car, barely able to move and had to hang onto a cloth strap attached to the car's headliner because my Oldsmobile was listing thirty degrees to starboard like the German pocket battleship, Graf Spee in

Montevideo harbor. Every time I drove into a dip in the road, the car's suspension bottomed out with a sickening clunk. The reason for the list and my uncomfortable position was the huge bulk of Carlo the mountain and a half, sitting beside me and hogging most of the front seat.

About thirty miles out of Barstow we lost the last pop music station on the car radio and were left with only singing cowboys and preachers. Carlo reached up a giant hand and switched off the radio. The silence was kind of nice but didn't last. Carlo the mountain and a half began to sing selections from his favorite operas in Italian at the top of his lungs. It wouldn't have been so bad if he had a good voice, but he didn't. His voice was like a cross between a steam shovel whistle and a water buffalo in labor.

The Brat: "Make him stop. That screeching sounds like we have a thousand cats in the back seat, all clawing on a chalkboard."

Captain Straight: "Yes, it is annoying."

I started looking ahead for the next diner or café to pull over and stop. My car still had that new car smell inside and I didn't want to smoke in it until that wonderful aroma faded away. Every hour or so after leaving Los Angeles I stopped the car so I could quickly suck down the smoke from two or three cigarettes to bring my nicotine levels back up to full. Carlo, on the other hand, didn't smoke, he ate. At every stop, we made he would enter a diner or café and emerge with a couple of hamburgers or hot dogs, sometimes both. Just past San Bernardino, I made the mistake of stopping at an isolated gas station that didn't offer food. I became alarmed when Carlo suddenly started hungrily eying the station attendant's dog. I had to distract and quickly hustle the mountain and a half back into the car before he could suck down the unfortunate animal in one huge bite. I regretted that I had no way to warn the various coyotes, rattlesnakes, lizards and horned toads inhabiting the surrounding desert that they were in mortal danger.

§

I had arrived at my office that morning at ten-thirty on the dot. Not surprisingly, Carlo was late. Gangsters are always late. It's a wonder to me how they managed to get all their gunmen assembled in that Chicago garage on time in order to pull off the St Valentine's day massacre. I'm sure there were some of them who arrived late, or forgot their bullets and missed all the fun. While I was waiting for the mountain and a half, I called Mrs. Adderley into my office.

"I have to go out of town for a few days," I told her, "and I don't want anything to change while I'm gone."

"Where are you going? I need to put it down in the logbook," she replied.

"What logbook, this is the first I've heard about a logbook."

"I've instituted a logbook for all the detectives. They must log their mileage and purpose for all their movements within and without the city."

"Mrs. Adderley," I asked, "how much do you know about your parents? Are they really your biological parents or are you may be the long lost illegitimate daughter of Josef Stalin and Laventiy Beria's more evil twin sister?"

"You can complain and make jokes all you want but I am determined to make this office efficient," said Mrs. Adderley stubbornly. It seemed that it was impossible for me to offend my office manager. But then again, power-obsessed people are usually thick-skinned.

"Okay, okay, but while I'm gone, no taking my company public and selling shares on the stock market or anything like that. And if you try to move this office while I'm gone, remember, I'm a detective. Even if you move it to a remote hellhole like, say, Tulsa, be assured I will track you down."

Carlo, the mountain and a half showed up at ten to eleven wearing a huge tropical suit with egg stains on his floral tie. We got in my Oldsmobile and set out. I took Wilshire east to Figueroa and then north to Pasadena where we turned right on Route 66 east. At Barstow, we turned left onto Route 91 north.

§

As we were nearing the dusty little town of Baker, Carlo dozed off and started clicking. With every drawn in breath he emitted an audible click.

The Brat: "First all the Dago singing and now he's clicking like an adding machine. Just take out your gun and shoot him. Look around you. There's plenty of places to hide the body."

Brat's proposal was the most ridiculous thing I had ever heard. Shooting Carlo would only make him really angry and being trapped in a sheet metal box traveling at sixty-eight miles per hour with an enraged Italian gangster the size of a Kodiak bear, was not on my list of thrills I wished to experience before I died. Instead of shooting the mountain and a half, or taking other drastic action, I decided to concentrate on something else to distract my brain from the clicks. I thought about the date I had with my girlfriend Billie the night before.

On our first date, I asked Billie why her father had given her a boy's name. She replied that she had four older sisters, and when her mother discovered she was pregnant again, her father declared that he was going to name the kid in the oven William, whatever sex the child turned out to be. This was an effort by Billie's father to try to back God into a corner and force the deity to give him a boy this time. The creator of heaven and earth, all matter and energy, man, elephants, tigers, and duck-billed platypuses, not to mention the time-space continuum, only chuckled and gave Billie's father another girl. After Billie's mother put her foot down, they named her Billie instead William.

I was really glad she had been born a girl. In her mid-twenties, Billie was about five foot two, with eyes of blue just like in that crappy old song. She had raven black hair, skin the color of fresh cream, dimples when she smiled, and a body that caused Little Matt to squirm and twitch all over in anticipation. Every time I was near her, the little tyrant would rush up to my head and demand to run things. This wasn't unusual. Most men do their thinking with their penises at one time or another. But sometimes Little Matt got so out of control, Captain Straight and I would have to lock him up in the cerebellum. The reason for Little Matt's frustration was Billie's teeny-weeny hang-up about sex before marriage. She was adamantly against it.

We met when I was testifying in a divorce case in old Judge Wilkerson's courtroom at the Superior Court downtown. Billie was the judge's court reporter. While on the stand one day, I looked over at her sitting in front of her machine and she returned a coquettish, sultry glance accompanied by a smile. I had been looked at like that by women many times and it usually meant: "Come hither handsome, I want to get to know you better."

I started hanging around the courthouse and flirting with Billie in my down-time. She had plenty of time to spend with me because her old judge usually spent his afternoons "working in chambers." What that actually meant was that he was sprawled on his couch, snoring off the effects of the five or six martinis he knocked back for lunch. So far, the old coot had proved that a human being could survive, even thrive, on a diet of nothing but vodka, a dash of vermouth and olives. His experience showed there was still hope for me with my much more pedestrian bourbon and peanut diet. Anyway, after several weeks of this rooster-hen like mating ritual, Billie consented to go out with me. Since then there had been many more dates.

The night before, I had taken her out to dinner, (The meal cost me $5.40 with tip, which I thought was outrageous.) and back to my apartment. As usual, I tried plying her with alcohol, which in the past I had found was very useful in crumbling the foundations of the locked gates on women's gardens of paradise. Billie declined, again as usual and we ended up doing what we always did, sitting on the sofa, holding each other and kissing with closed mouths. Little Matt became excited and rose to the occasion, but soon became frustrated.

Little Matt: "Would you stop with all the endless kissing? Can't you see that I'm ready to explode here? Why don't you try to cop a feel? Maybe she'll let you this time."

I inched my right hand toward her left breast slowly and carefully, like the Green hornet sneaking up on Doctor Frenzy. In response, Billie stiffened and pulled away from me.

"We've been through this many times, not until I have a ring on my third finger left hand and we are on our wedding night," she said as she removed my hand from the vicinity of her breast. "Why don't we discuss what our children's names are going to be?"

At the suggestion of marriage and children, Little Matt shrank faster than President Truman's prospects for reelection. But the little bastard wasn't always so skittish about marriage. When Billie first brought it up on one of our earlier dates, Little Matt was all for it, thinking that it would be an easy way to Billie's charms. Then it began to dawn on him that marriage meant monogamy and he back-peddled faster than Cat Woman after mistakenly strolling into the Westminster dog show.

Little Matt: "I mean it ain't natural. Men need to sow their seed around like honeybees buzzing from flower to flower spreading pollen. We have to ensure the survival of the species. It all goes back to caveman days when so many guys were getting gobbled up by saber-tooth tigers."

The Brat: "That's good Little Matt, just what we wanted, an anthropology lesson delivered by a moron. Maybe we could get you a job as a guest lecturer at UCLA. But all the nubile young coeds walking around in their tight sweaters would get you so excited you'd flame out in fifteen minutes and have to be carried off-campus on a stretcher."

Captain Straight: "That's enough."

The Brat: "It would be fun though, to listen to a faculty member introduce you at one of your lectures. 'Ladies and gentlemen, today's lecture on the mysterious disappearance of the Anasazi culture will be delivered by Matt Cole's penis. And I must warn any squeamish young ladies in the audience, Mr. Cole's penis may spring erect at any time for no discernible reason.'"

Little Matt: "Okay, okay, just leave me alone."

I wasn't ready to give up on steering Billie into bed just yet. I tried reasoning with her.

"You know," I began, "we have to approach this problem logically. When I go into that little deli over on Melrose for some sliced ham, my friend Maury always gives me the first slice as a sample, just to see if I'll like it. He doesn't make me buy a whole pig just to get a sample of ham. And when I bought my new car, the salesman didn't expect me to buy it sight unseen, but let me test drive it first. It's perfectly logical and the way of the modern world. I mean what if we tie the knot only to discover on our wedding night that our parts don't fit together correctly? What if I'm a slot and you're a Phillips? Or you're a slot and I'm a Phillips?"

"If you're trying to convince me to take off my clothes, comparing me to a screwdriver isn't the way to do it, trust me," replied Billie.

"Okay, how about this. You have to be more adventurous. After Betsy Ross got done stitching up the new flag for the

Continental Army, she went right out and helped storm the Bastille with one naked breast hanging out…"

"Hold on," interrupted Billie, "the Bastille is in Paris, and that was the French Revolution, not the American, nice try."

"See, I blame the American educational system. If your teachers at school hadn't been so damn conscientious in teaching you history, that last line might have worked."

"I'm sorry Matt, but until I have a gold ring on my third finger left hand and a marriage license safely tucked away in a safe deposit box, there will be no sex, not even an itty-bitty sample. You know the line from the Chinese laundry: "no-tickee, no washee?" Well, with me it's no ringee, no Billie."

She suddenly stopped talking and sniffed the air. "This place stinks, when are you going to clean up this pigsty?"

"I can't do that, it would ruin my system," I replied.

"System, what pray tell is your "system?"

"I did some time and motion studies and realized that it was much more efficient to store dishes dirty in the sink, than clean in the cupboard. It takes twenty-six minutes to wash, dry and put away a sink full of dishes. On the other hand, you can wash one plate and fork in less than thirty seconds if you use the rough skin on the ball of your thumb as a scrubber and your thumbnail to scrape away the stubborn pieces. And that's just the kitchen. I find it more efficient to just buy new sheets for the bed every few months than to go through the hassle of washing them," I replied.

"I can see there need to be big changes around here."

The Brat: "I bet Hitler said much the same thing while he was gazing across the Polish border in 1939."

My girlfriend's unreasonable obstinacy about perfectly normal biological functions and her neatness fetish was causing my frustration level to rise into the danger zone. The problem was that Billie was my only outlet for female companionship at that time. All bachelors go through dry spells, but brother, this one was a doozie and I couldn't understand why. Having just turned thirty-one I was still reasonably good looking if I do say so myself. I was six foot tall with a slim, lanky frame and was blessed with a mass of dark brown wavy hair. My facial features were regular, with nothing too big or too small to stand out and ruin the effect. My complexion was darker than usual but I didn't think that was my problem. It was all so perplexing. In the past, arid patches wouldn't bother me so much because I always had Gracie.

A few months after I returned to the United States from Guadalcanal, I moved into a rooming house run by a woman named Mrs. Hudson. Soon after, I embarked on a torrid affair with a fellow tenant. She was a single school teacher in her forties named Gracie. The affair continued for a long time.

Then one evening in early 1946, Gracie was conducting parent-teacher conferences with the parents of her second-grade students. Library tables were set up in the school gym for the conferences. A widower in his early fifties walked up to Gracie's table and introduced himself as the grandfather of one of her students. At the precise moment when the two locked eyes, a violent earthquake occurred. The ground shook. Pictures and maps and other shit fell from the walls and dust filtered down from the rafters. The funny thing was, though, was that when the shaking stopped, both Gracie and the man looked around and noticed that nobody else in the room had felt the earthquake and were carrying on normally. Soon after, Gracie ended our affair and announced she was getting married. I tried to reason with her and get her to continue our little arrangement until the marriage ceremony, just for continuity's sake and to keep her in practice, but she said no and dropped me like a two-week old boiled egg.

After I took Billie home after our date, Little Matt was the only one of my voices who made a comment.

Little Matt: "Oh hell. I guess we struck out again. But, that's why we keep that fur glove, for emergencies like this."

I was aroused from my memories when Carlo and I drove between two big hills and I saw the town of Las Vegas ahead. Soon I would find out why Tony Cardello had me dragged up there. Maybe it was some simple thing like he lost one of his gold cufflinks and he wanted me to find it, but I didn't think so.

CHAPTER FOUR

LAS VEGAS
JUNE 6, 1947
4:40 P.M.

A s I looked through my windshield at the medium-sized dusty town in the distance, I wondered what had possessed anyone to build a town there. I mean, the terrain was all wrong for human habitation. The burg was built on a flat desert plain with mountains to the west that rose steeply to ten thousand feet or so. Wind blowing over those mountains would rapidly accelerate as it rushed down the mountainsides onto the plain. I bet that the place was windy most of the time. In the summer the wind would be hot and arid, and even when the wind didn't blow, you would be baked like a casserole by the hot desert sun. In the winter, however, the same wind would flow over the snow on the mountains and turn so cold your left testicle would turn black from frostbite and fall off. Your right testicle and your Johnson wouldn't be affected because they had already been frozen off the previous winter. Then I sighed. Because so many of the decisions humans make are illogical, the founding of Las Vegas was probably just a fluke. Maybe this was where a wandering prospector's mule suddenly dropped dead, and he decided to stay awhile and build a shack.

Carlo, who had been dozing, woke up and decided to stretch. His elbow, nestled for the last hour against my right ribcage, suddenly squashed me tighter against the driver's door making it impossible for me to breathe. Thankfully, the poke in the ribs was only fleeting and the pressure eased as the mountain and a half sat up straight in the seat. We were still on US Route 91, headed toward the cluster of buildings of downtown Las Vegas about four or five miles ahead. We were driving through flat desert land, with nothing but sagebrush and tumbleweeds visible in the barren landscape.

"That's the Flamingo, ahead on the right," said Carlo.

As we got closer I could see that The Flamingo was a large, long building, built of tan stone (or concrete made to look like tan stone) with dark brown trim. A tall, narrow sign looking similar to an Egyptian obelisk of the same stone material rose vertically from the roof. It had the hotel's name spelled out vertically on it with large metal letters bolted to the stone. At the top of the sign was a stylized image of a bright pink flamingo. I thought that this oblong building must be the casino and restaurant. Behind this structure were several large three-story blocks of buildings constructed of the same tan stone. These had to be the joint's hotel rooms. An asphalt parking lot occupied the sixty-yards or so of distance between the highway and the casino. I looked around. There were no other buildings around the Flamingo

Hotel. The landscape around it was as barren and lifeless as Tallulah Bankhead's movie career.

I turned right into the parking lot and Carlo directed me to the south end of the casino building. He motioned for me to follow a driveway that led under an overhang supported on its weak side by thick metal poles. A horizontal sign above the overhand advertised: CASINO-LOUNGE- RESTAURANT. I drove under the overhang and parked. A young parking attendant ran up and opened my door so I could get out and stretch. He also gave me a parking ticket and started to replace me behind the wheel, but abruptly stopped in his tracks when he saw Carlo the mountain and a half, looking as large as King Kong's older big brother, still sprawled on the front seat. Slowly, Carlo got out on the passenger side. The heavy car returned to level and I swore I heard my Oldsmobile give a sigh of relief, but maybe I imagined it. The wall of the casino separating it from the carport were all glass, floor to ceiling. The swinging doors were also of glass and over an inch thick. Carlo and I walked into the casino side by side like old pals.

The décor was modern, all stone, glass and sharp angles on a huge scale. The whole room was carpeted in red with some kind of squiggly design in blue on it that made me kind of dizzy to look at. To my immediate right was a bank of slot machines. In fact, there were slot machines tucked into every corner of available space at the edges of the lobby. Further along on my right was the entrance to the lounge. There was a prominently placed display board showcasing the featured singers, dancers or,

I don't know, jugglers, performing there. To my right was a long bar with about twenty leather-covered backless stools pushed up against it. Across the lobby, I saw some steps leading up to a landing on which were two enormous concrete pillars ascending to the roof. These pillars framed the doorway to the casino. Through this entrance, I could see craps tables, roulette wheels, blackjack tables, and bank after bank of one-armed bandits. The place was moderately busy but I imagined that later in the evening the casino would be packed with Californians, it being Friday night and the start of the weekend.

Carlo told me to stay in place and not go wandering off while he went to get Tony. I sat down on one of the backless stools at the bar. Within two minutes a good looking waitress with large breasts appeared in a skimpy outfit and asked if I wanted a free welcome drink.

Little Matt: "Well, what have we here? Look at those knockers."

Having never in my life passed up a free drink, I ordered a double Jack Daniels neat. Her large breasts must have been phony and instead housed containers full of bourbon because within about a minute she was back with my drink. I gave her a dollar tip and I could tell by the expression on her face when she turned away that she thought I was a cheapskate.

I sat there at the bar and sipped my bourbon and occupied myself by watching in the mirror over the bar as an old granny behind me pushed coins into a slot machine. She fed in nickels with the same single-minded purpose as a Marine machine gunner repulsing a Japanese Bonzai charge on Guadalcanal.

"Well, Peeper, it's been a long time, said a voice behind me. I turned around on the barstool and there was Tony Cardello, with Carlo the mountain and a half towering behind him. Tony looked about the same as I had last seen him three years ago. A few more grey hairs and maybe some new wrinkles around the eyes, but he was still the Tony I remembered. He was tall and fit, in his early forties with a handsome, dark Mediterranean face and confident, even cocky air. His three hundred dollar double-breasted suit was perfectly tailored. He took my hand and shook it warmly like we were old pals. Tony was smiling, Carlo was smiling, so I smiled too.

The Brat: "It might be well for you to remember that these gangsters are not your friends. They're acting all buddy-buddy because they want something from you. And if you don't deliver what they want, you may find yourself ventilated and at the bottom of an abandoned mine shaft."

"How do you like our little operation here," said Tony, "cost six million to build."

"Impressive," I replied. In truth, I wasn't that impressed. Gambling was for rubes. In most gambling joints the roulette wheels were rigged and the slot machines were set to only deliver big jackpots to the shills for the house. If you were to have a run of luck at cards, the house goons would run you out quicker than a hobo that sneaked into the Vanderbilt mansion.

"We built this place to have class. All the other joints in town are all western dives with guys wearing chaps and ten-gallon hats meeting you at the door and saying shit like 'Howdy pardner.' Our place is like a classy club on the Sunset Strip in L.A."

"C'mon up to my office," said Tony," I got a little job I want you to do." The smile had disappeared from his face. I followed him across the lobby to an unmarked door with Carlo the mountain and a half bringing up the rear. The opened door revealed a staircase going up. I hobbled up the stairs after Tony, holding onto the handrail, and then we trudged down a long dark hallway. Then we entered an enormous room where a bunch of hoods sat around looking through one-way glass panels at the gameplay in the casino below. Tony led me through another unmarked door to a cramped office. We sat down separated by a small desk and Carlo stood with his back to the wall off to the side.

After pouring two stiff shots of scotch whiskey into two glasses and sliding one across the table to me, Tony Cardello took out his wallet, pulled out a small photograph and handed it to me. It was a likeness of a pretty, smiling young woman with dark Italian features and dark hair worn down off her shoulders.

"That's my sister Carmen," began Tony, "she's twenty years old. About six months ago she began to chafe under the control of our domineering mother in New Jersey. She came out here to live with me for a while. One day Carmen met Ben Siegel as he was strolling through the casino. She fell for his pretty face and took up with him. Now, I wasn't that concerned, I thought it would be just a brief fling. Ben doesn't stay with his girlfriends very long, and I never knowed a woman to be hurt by a little screwing."

"Then three weeks ago Ben took my sister on a trip to California with him, and for some reason, she stayed there. I didn't like it, but there wasn't much I could do. On weekends Ben stays with his girlfriend, Virginia Hill, in her rented mansion in Beverly hills. If Ben's girlfriends were like the German army then Virginia would be Field Marshal Rommel if you get my drift. Since Carmen left I talked to her a couple of times on the phone and she seemed okay. She said she was staying in a room over the garage in Virginia's mansion and managing Ben's appointment schedule. Then a week ago, Carmen called me crying. She said Ben had beaten her up pretty bad. I told her to call a cab and get the hell out of there and wired her enough dough via Western Union to ride a train back here."

"I didn't hear anything more until three days ago when Ben himself called me into his office here at the Flamingo. He said that Carmen had stolen a diamond bracelet from Virginia Hill and had run off with it. I didn't buy it then and I'm not buying it now. My mama back in New Jersey is having fits, sending me wires twice and three times a day. The job I want you to do is to go back to L.A. and find my sister," said Tony.

"Let me get this straight, you want me to snoop around Bugsy Siegel's girlfriend's house, which is probably guarded be fifty jumpy guys armed with Tommy guns, and try to find your missing sister?"

"Right. I'm not in a position to do it and neither is Carlo."

Captain Straight: " Oh, no no no no no no..."

"Well, Tony," I said as I stood up, "nice to see you again and thanks for the drink and the tour of your operation here, but I have to get back to Los Angeles. My car needs servicing and I really ought to get a haircut...?'

"SIT DOWN!" Tony interrupted me loudly and I sat. "First off, if you use that nickname 'Bugsy' within the hearing of anyone else around here but Carlo and me, you'll be dead within five minutes and at the bottom of an abandoned mineshaft within thirty more. Ben Siegel hates that nickname."

The Brat: "See? I was right about the mineshaft."

"I'm not asking you to go to Virginia Hill's house cold. We got you an in," said Tony in a much calmer voice.

"An in, what kind of an in?" I asked.

"If you'll shut the fuck up for a second, I'll tell you," said Tony, "you know, you got the biggest yap of any non-organization guy I know."

Tony looked over at Carlo and pointed at his face. "Take a gander at that mug. To look at him you would think he didn't have two brain cells to rub together, right?"

"I think Carlo looks very intelligent, and he's handsome too," I retorted.

"SHUT UP!" yelled Tony. "Carlo works at Virginia Hill's mansion as a bodyguard, and Virginia, for some strange reason, has taken a shine to him. Nothing sexual you understand, but it's like he's her pet elephant or something. When the diamond bracelet and my sister disappeared Virginia reported the disappearance of the bracelet to the police. The two detectives who came out to the mansion just wandered around the property for twenty minutes, stole two leftover fried chicken legs from the refrigerator in the kitchen and then drove away. Virginia was fit to be tied and was raving about how useless the cops were. Then my cousin Carlo here, using more brainpower than I thought he had, piped up and told Virginia that he knowed a peeper who was very good at finding missing things. So, the upshot is, Virginia, is prepared to hire you to find her missing bracelet."

"So I have Carlo to thank for this wonderful opportunity? Carlo, you don't have any more little jobs you would recommend me for? Maybe disarming dud bombs in the ruins of Berlin, or defanging some King Cobras?"

Carlo just shook his head and gave me a weird look, kind of like he was trying to figure out if I was mocking him or not.

Captain straight: "Go ahead and mock a three hundred pound gorilla whose idea of fun is to turn six-foot guys into three-foot guys by folding them like an accordion. Are you nuts?"

I turned back to Tony Cardello. " Tony, I really think that you got the wrong guy for this job. I'm a crippled peeper, and I'm not really equipped for work on a case like this."

Tony didn't reply but just stared at me. We locked eyes for twenty seconds, during which His stare got harder and harder. Finally, I couldn't take it anymore. I didn't have much of a choice, I had to take on the job.

"I interpret your hostile stare to mean that I should just shut the hell up and go find your missing sister, and if I refuse, you'll have Carlo here pinch off my head and bury me out in some canyon in the desert. "

"Exactly, now you're getting the picture," replied Tony.

"Okay, I'll look into it. I charge a hundred bucks a day plus expenses." I replied.

"Shit, Peeper, that's pretty steep."

Another trait of gangsters was that they were incredibly stingy with their own money, and had been known to haggle with shoeshine boys over the price of a buff.

'If that's too much money, we can always just forget the whole thing. I can go back to L.A. and we'll call it square," I said brightly.

"Not a chance, I'll pay, but I don't like it."

"Have you considered the possibility that Carmen may be guilty of stealing the bracelet, then got scared and ran off?" I asked.

"My sister Carmen has a cute face and a good body with overdeveloped mammary glands, but...

"What are mammary glands Tony," Carlo interrupted to ask.

"TITTIES, Carlo, TITTIES!" shouted Tony.

"Anyway," Tony continued after the interruption, " Carmen is good looking, but no one has ever accused her of being bright. When God was passing out brains, she was standing in the tit line filing her nails. She's like a fourteen-year-old girl emotionally and reads true romance magazines by the gross. If Carmen did steal that bracelet, it was because some son of a bitch she thought she was in love with put her up to it."

"Okay, I'll drive back to Los Angeles tomorrow morning and start. Any chance of getting a free room at the Flamingo for the night? I asked.

"Bullshit. You ain't staying the night," said Tony Cardello. "You have to get back to L.A. tonight so you can rest up. Carlo here has made an appointment for you with Virginia Hill for one in the afternoon tomorrow to start investigating her missing bracelet. It's Okay, Carlo can help you with the driving. It's one of the two things he does well. The other thing he's good at is taking care of wise-ass peepers who tell me they'll do something and then don't do it."

The Brat: "Now I know how Louis XVI felt just before he suddenly went from five feet six to four feet seven."

CHAPTER FIVE

LOS ANGELES
JUNE 7, 1947
SATURDAY
10:30 A.M.

I was turning left from Fairfax Avenue onto Wilshire I saw a billboard high up on the corner opposite me. It was about thirty feet by twenty in size. It featured a stylishly dressed woman with a pensive expression on her face. Underneath the woman, the lettering read: "ARE YOU SURE YOUR HUSBAND IS BEING FAITHFUL TO YOU? IF YOU WANT TO KNOW FOR SURE, CONTACT THE A-1 DISCREET DETECTIVE AGENCY- CALL WI 6-4532.

Being already irritable that Saturday morning, the sight of the billboard put me over the edge. I stormed into my detective agency and confronted a twitching, frightened Betty at her counter. She already had her purse and other junk set out on the counter in preparation for leaving. The office was only open until twelve on Saturdays.

"Buzz the Witch of Endor and tell her to meet me in my office," I said none too kindly.

Betty's eyes grew wide as saucers and her mouth was agape. "Witch of Endor?" she choked out.

"Contact Mrs. Adderley and tell her to join me in my private office post-haste," I said in a much more calm and phony nice voice.

I went directly to my private office and immediately violated my resolution to only drink bourbon from a glass. In fact, I violated it twice in the space of three minutes. Shortly after, Mrs. Adderley breezed defiantly in, followed by the ever-present Luann. Luann was so close behind her boss that if Mrs. Adderley made a sudden turn she would break her nose.

"I thought I told you not to change anything while I was gone. I just saw the billboard at Fairfax and Wilshire," I said menacingly.

"Yes, there is one there and at seventeen other locations about the city. The one you saw features a woman. Others show a man wondering about the faithfulness of his wife," said Mrs. Adderley speaking as if she was communicating with an imbecile.

Captain Straight: "You forgot to lock your gun in the bottom drawer. I suggest that you calm down and don't do anything rash."

The Brat: "Oh I don't know, with one well-placed shot you might be able to get two for one and drill both of them. But you'll have to time your shot just right, Luann ducks and weaves better than Joe Louis."

"Why wasn't I told about this?"

"I did tell you," said my office manager patiently, "all the information about our new ad campaign was in the inter-office memo I sent you."

"Wait a minute, what inter-office memo? Since when do we have inter-office memos?" I asked.

"Oh, I instituted the procedure of communicating important matters in inter-office memos about a month ago. It allows us to keep a permanent record of all important decisions. I sent you an inter-office memo explaining all about it," replied Mrs. Adderley. As she stepped forward and began rifling through the stack of papers in my "In" tray, my right hand started inching toward my holstered gun.

"See, it's all explained right here," she said as she handed me two sheets of paper. The pages were indeed labeled as inter-office memos. One instituted the policy of inter-office memos themselves and the other explained the advertising campaign.

"I don't think you understand how this is supposed to work," I said. " You're supposed to come to me and say, 'Hi boss, I've got this really great idea for an advertising campaign and I'm really anxious to hear what you think about my great new idea.' Then we discuss it and come to some sort of an agreement."

"That's what I was doing in the inter-office memo. Since I didn't get an inter-office memo back from you with your input, I went ahead on my own. Really Mr. Cole, sometimes I wonder if you pay enough attention to your business. It might help if you spend a little less time swilling bourbon in your private office."

"Okay, that's all on this subject right now, Mrs. Adderley. We'll talk about this again at another time. There's something else. I'm going to be working off the books on a special private case for a few days. So, I will be in and out of the office at irregular times. But rest assured, I'll call in at regular intervals so Betty can read to me the contents of the latest, hot off the presses inter-office memos."

"What is the nature of this 'special case?' Whom does it involve and to whom do we send the bill for your services? Mr. Cole, this is decidedly irregular." Mrs. Adderley was suddenly upset that I was keeping her in the dark about something I was doing and I relished it.

"I'm not telling you. Now you know how it feels," I said with a smile and a wink as I brought out my bourbon bottle and glass.

After the office manager left in a huff, I lit up a Camel and sipped my drink. Despite seven hours of sleep, I was still tired from the five hundred mile drive I had completed the day before. Tony Cardello had assured me that Carlo would help me with the driving but he didn't. After a heavy meal in the Flamingo restaurant, the mountain and a half climbed in the back seat of my car and promptly started to snore and fart in his sleep all the way to Los Angeles. Carlo's bulk caused the rear of my new Oldsmobile to squat on its springs and point the nose of the car at the sky. This wasn't much of a problem in daylight but became one when the sunset and it became dark. I had to deal with drivers going the other way angrily flashing their lights at me all the way home.

We only stopped once, in Barstow for gas. Carlo the mountain and a half probably ate every morsel of food available in a roadside diner before going back to sleep. When we got back to Los Angeles, Carlo asked to be let off downtown. Before he climbed out of my car, he handed me a claim-ticket from a self-park lot over on Pico. On the back was written Virginia Hill's Beverly Hills address.

My intercom buzzed. I hit the correct button the first time. Maybe I was catching on to this big-shot executive routine.

"Mr. Cole, there's a man out here who wants to speak to you. He won't give his name."

I thought it was probably a potential client who wasn't sure he really wanted to hire a detective and was acting shy. In any case, I wasn't about to let someone into my private office who wouldn't identify himself, at least until I got a good look at him first. I limped out the door of my office, down the short hall and turned the corner into the reception area. I looked at the man standing in front of Betty's counter and stopped dead in my tracks in shock.

The guy was dressed in a finely tailored double-breasted gray suit and was holding a gray felt hat in his hands. Except for his blondish gray hair and the unhealthy pallor of his skin, it might have been an older version of myself, arrived from twenty-five years in the future. I instantly knew who the person was. His name was Robert Matthew Cole, my dear old dad, who had abandoned my mother and I when I was six years old. A flood of emotions roiled my gut as I stood there. The first was white hit anger, I hated the son of a bitch.

The Brat: "Take out your gun and shoot that bastard!"

Captain Straight: " Hold on, Matt, he's not worth killing. Just throw him down the stairs."

The memories came flooding back. After my father deserted us, for the first two weeks or so I arrived home from school each day eagerly expecting that when I arrived home my daddy would be there and everything would be as it was before. But he didn't come back and then the guilt set in. I felt that I must have done something bad to drive him away. I was a good for nothing son. As I thought of the nights that I cried myself to sleep and the rejection I felt for the next few years, my stomach turned sour with bile. Next, I thought of the years my mother and I spent in cheap, shabby two-room flats with me helping her wash our laundry in the kitchen sink and hanging it out to dry on makeshift clotheslines outside. I thought of the skimpy meals and the ragged clothes I had to wear to school. Over the years my agony of emotional pain gradually changed into disgust, hostility, and resentment. My father was dead to me.

"You have a lot of nerve to walk in here, you bastard," I said to him across the fifteen feet or so of space between us. My words came out as a raspy croak. My father returned a sheepish look then looked down at the floor for a moment. Then his eyes came up again and gazed at me. I could tell he was in pain too.

"Matthew, I know you hate me and I don't blame you, but I have to talk to you. Give me ten minutes of your time and you never have to see me again," he said.

"Forget it. I'm not interested in anything you have to say. Just get the hell out of here before I forcibly eject you."

"I'm sorry son, but I'm going to stay here on one of these couches until you talk to me."

"Suit yourself, but it'll be a cold day in hell before I say another word to you," I said and turned on my heel and went back to my private office to consume several shots of Jack Daniel's Old No.7 Whiskey and chain smoke Camel cigarettes.

CHAPTER SIX

BEVERLY HILLS
JUNE 7, 1947
SATURDAY
12:45 P.M.

As seen from the front seat of my car parked at the curb in front, the house at 810 N. Linden Drive, Beverly Hills, was pink, big and imposing. Way too large for its lot, the house had been built in the "Moorish Castle" style that had been popular with some movie stars and other bigshots in the twenties. There was a capped turret in the front, the roofline was stepped and the windows were topped with pointed arches. It was meant to suggest the mystique of old Bagdad and "A thousand and one Arabian nights." To my skeptical eye, it didn't look like a Moorish castle or even a normal house, but only ridiculous and pretentious. To cap it off there was a big, ugly pagoda-like structure in the front yard. It was made out of lattice and painted a darker shade of pink than the one on the house. There were two chairs and a small table inside. I had about ten minutes to kill before my one P.M. appointment with Virginia

Hill. I used the time to thinks about everything I had learned
about her when I was an LAPD cop before the war.

She called herself an actress but the only motion picture part
she ever played was as an uncredited hat check girl in the 1941
movie, "Manpower." It wasn't hard to imagine how she had got
the part. She had once publicly performed oral sex on every male
present at a mob dinner party on a dare. Born in some backward,
rural shithole in Alabama, by rights she should have ended up
illiterate, and barefoot with platoons of kids clinging to her
ragged skirts. Instead, while still in her teens, she surfaced in
Chicago as a gangster's moll and party girl. Virginia somehow
rose rapidly in the underworld of the Chicago mob and into
positions of more responsibility. She was known as a dame with
brains who could keep her mouth shut. She met Bugsy Siegel in
1937 and the two were instantly consumed with lust for each
other. Their stormy, on-again, off-again New York affair was the
talk of the mob underworld, not to mention the gossip columns
of the newspapers. When Siegel moved to Los Angeles in 1938,
Virginia came too and using Bugsy's money rented the big, ugly
mansion to be near him.

At one on the dot, I got out of my car and started up the
concrete walkway toward the front door. To my left, across an
expanse of lawn, I could see a driveway running parallel to the
walkway that led under a portico at the north end of the house,
and then presumably continued on to garages in the back.

The Brat: " It's still not too late to drive to San Pedro and sign on as a crewmember of a tramp steamer headed to the Far-East."

Captain Straight: "It would probably be healthier than going in that front door."

Little Matt: "Yeah, maybe the ship will end up in Tahiti. I hear the girls there walk around with their tits hanging out."

I stopped in front of the front door, which was a massive affair capped by a pointed arch. I rang the bell and waited. While I stood there I looked up and down the street. Big houses on small lots stretched away from me on both sides and across the street. They were most likely occupied by wealthy executives from the movie industry, nearby aircraft manufacturers and fat cat politicians. I could picture how scandalized they were when they found out a notorious gangster and his moll had moved in among them.

The door was answered by a hatchet-faced maid in her fifties who had all the welcoming grace of a German machine-gunner at Omaha Beach. "What do you want?" she growled through the partially opened door.

" Yes, I have a one o'clock appointment with Virginia Hill..."

My response to the maid was cut short when the door was wrenched fully open and a muscular, hard-looking man with slicked-back dark hair appeared. He was in his forties wearing suit trousers and shirtsleeves and a thirty-eight revolver in a brown leather shoulder holster.

"Whatsoever you are sellin', we don't want any," he said in standard gangland patois. He was probably a recent graduate of the "Dutch" Shultz Memorial charm school in Brooklyn.

"I have a one o'clock appointment with Virginia Hill. I'm a private detective," I replied and handed him one of my business cards.

"Private dick huh? What's Virginia need with a private dick?" said the gangster as he stared at the inscription on my card. Whether he could actually read the words on the card was an open question.

"I won't know that until I talk to her. She called me."

"All right smart ass, come on in here," he said and ushered me into the smallish entry area. The thug expertly patted me down and took my gun from its holster. He roughly shoved my Colt into his front waistband. Now, this was a moronic thing to do with a Colt Government Model pistol. If there was a round in the chamber and the thumb safety was off as many people including me carried it, the grip safety happened to be accidentally depressed by the web of his hand as he was shoving the gun down his pants, and the trigger snagged on a fold of cloth or something, then the fool would be singing soprano in the prison choir the next time he went up to the big house.

The interior of the house was about as impressive as the exterior. I could see that a lack of maintenance was taking its toll on the inside. There were cracks in the crown molding lining the ceiling, the paint on the walls was scratched and worn, and the furnishings, though once costly, were now definitely shabby. Houses were a lot like people. Without constant maintenance, both old people and old houses deteriorate quickly.

From the entry hall, the gangster walked me by the arm to a doorway on the opposite wall from the front door, down a long hallway and into the kitchen. Upon entering the big white room, I saw Carlo the mountain and a half, seated on two chairs at a big table. He had his coat off like the other gangster, and I could see he was similarly armed with what looked like a .45 automatic in a shoulder holster. Carlo had a napkin tucked into the collar of his shirt and was eating an enormous sandwich that looked like it was made by slicing a whole loaf of French bread lengthwise and then piling in about twenty pounds of meatballs, marinara sauce, and parmesan cheese. When he saw me he didn't react or act like he knew me. He just looked up at the other hood with an expression of curiosity. It began to dawn on me that maybe Carlo the mountain and a half wasn't as dumb as he let on and his cousin Tony said. I would have to keep that in mind in the future.

"Dis bird says he's a private dick. He says Virginia called him and wants to see him. You know anything 'bout dis?" said the hoodlum who had my pistol in his waistband pointed at his balls with a live round in the chamber.

"Yeah, Solly, Virginia is still all hot and bothered bout her missing bracelet. She got in touch with this guy to find it. He's okay I think," said Carlo the mountain and a half, pointing at me, "Tony and me had dealings with him before over some stolen organization money."

" Okee-dokee, if you think he's square, I'll take him upstairs ta Virginia, but if Ben raises a squawk, it'll be on you, not me," replied the gangster. Carlo just nodded. The man I now knew was named Solly walked me up the stairs and down another hallway to a door at the end, where he knocked sharply.

"WHAT?" screamed a female voice through the door.

"GOT ME A PRIVATE DICK HERE WHO SAYS YOU WANTS TO SEE HIM," yelled back Sol.

" LET HIM IN," screamed the female voice.

The Brat: "Why do you think they're yelling like that? Maybe they're hard of hearing."

I was escorted into the room. It turned out to be a dressing room that connected to a bedroom next door. Sitting at a mirrored vanity with her back to me was a woman with dark hair which she was brushing with a mother-of-pearl backed brush. She put the brush down, stood and turned around.

Virginia Hill was about thirty and was tall for a woman. She had long, shapely showgirl legs and was wearing what looked like a negligee covered by an untied robe. Her oval-shaped face was framed by dark brown hair worn shoulder length. Her cream-colored skin looked unlined, but I suspected that wouldn't be the case up close. A person couldn't have led the life she had without some major wear and tear on her drivetrain. Her bright red lipstick complemented her dark features, but her mascara accented eyes were the giveaway to what was inside. I last time I had seen eyes that hard were those of a fanatical Japanese soldier who was charging at me wanting to skewer me with a bayonet. Still, all in all, if you didn't look too closely, she was a good looking woman. Little Matt certainly thought so. He began to stir and rise to the occasion.

Captain Straight: "Oh no you don't you little bastard. Don't you know how dangerous this lady is? She'll cut you off, balls and all and leave you flopping on the floor like a beached mackerel."

The imagery contained in the captain's words caused Little Matt to shrivel like the Dow Jones average on Black Tuesday.

"Okay, Solly, you can go and leave us alone," said Virginia Hill. I could detect the remnants of a southern drawl in her speech.

"Ah, now Virginia, you knows the boss says I can't leave you in a room alone wit a gent?"

Virginia Hill's face contorted with rage faster than a V-2 rocket leaving the launch pad. "You tell Ben Siegel that he can't tell me what to do in my own house. He doesn't fucking own me! Get the fuck out!"

"C'mon Virginia, You're puttin' me on a spot here."

Virginia Hill suddenly picked up a figurine from a side table and hurled it at Solly. Unfortunately, I was between her and her target like a goose innocently flying into the arc of a mortar shell, directly in her line of fire.

Captain Straight: "Duck!" And I did.

The Brat: "Ah, the typical American gangland family, can't you feel the love."

The figurine smashed against the wall a foot from Solly's head. "Okay, okay, I'll go, but you havta tell Ben it was not my fault. You made me leave you alone wit dis bird."

After Solly left and closed the door, Virginia pointed to a sofa and we both sat at opposite ends like strangers on a first date looking at each other.

"I understand you want my help in finding a missing bracelet," I offered.

"That's why I arranged with the big guy for you to come here. I hope you have more brains than the idiots already trying to find it."

"Can you describe the bracelet?"

"Yeah, it is three-quarters of an inch wide, solid platinum and has four rows of one half carat Asscher cut diamonds on it. About midway along the band, the rows of diamonds are interrupted by a diamond pattern done in rubies as an accent. It has a replacement silver clasp because the platinum one broke a few years ago. A friend a mine from Chicago, Joey Epstein, gave the bracelet to me. He said it was worth ten grand, but all men lie. I figure it's worth seven. But I want to get it back because it has sentimental value, you see?"

"Where did you store the bracelet and when did it go missing?"

"I kept it in my jewelry box in my bedroom. I noticed it was missing eight days ago, May, 30th. I tried to get Ben to look into the theft but he acted like it was no big deal and laughed about it. Next, I called the police, The two idiots they sent out here couldn't find their dicks with both hands even if there was a big red arrow with flashing lights on it pointing to their little shriveled weenies."

"Before May, 31st, when was the last time you saw the bracelet in your jewelry box?" I asked.

"I wore the bracelet out to dinner on the Saturday before, May 24th."

"So we have a three-day window in which the theft occurred. Can you remember anything unusual happening about that time? Did any of your employees not show up for work? Anyone unusual having access to your bedroom?"

"No. No one had access to my bedroom except me, Ben and my maid Bertha. Bertha is reliable and has been with me for years. She won't steal from me because she knows that I will cleave her with an ax right down to her belly button if she ever takes anything from me or tells tales out of school. As to people disappearing, the only one I can think of is that stupid little Italian bitch Carmen. Ben told me she was his California appointments secretary and stashed her in one of the little rooms over the garage. Appointment secretary my ass. She was just another of Ben's concubines. When he was here on weekends and I was out of the house shopping or something, he used to sneak up to her little room for a quick blow job. Ben and I had a fight over her because I didn't appreciate him putting her up here in my house. Anyway, Carmen disappeared the day I discovered the bracelet missing. The only other person who made himself scarce about that time was the kid I hired as a gardener, but he didn't have a room here. About two days after the bracelet came up missing, he called Solly on the phone and quit. Now the grass is ass high to a giraffe in the back yard."

"Do you think Carmen could have taken the bracelet?"

"I don't think so. She was a stupid, mousy little bitch who was afraid of her own shadow and never came into the house. Ben thinks she might be involved but I don't." replied Virginia.

"Did the gardener who quit have access to the house?"

"No. he was strictly limited to the outside grounds," replied Virginia, lighting up a cigarette with a silver lighter.

"You called him a "kid." How old was he?"

"I don't know, maybe twenty. I called him a kid because he was like a cute, all American boy type. You know, like with crew-cut hair and jeans, and he was always saying shit like, 'gee-whiz' and 'golly' and whistling while he mowed the yard."

"What is his name?"

"Beats the shit outa me, somethin' like, Billy or Bobby maybe."

"I'm going to need to speak with all your servants. Sometimes they know things that their employers don't," I said.

Virginia shrugged, "I gotta cook, she's an old bat named Ethel. She has a face that looks like somebody real mad rearranged with a crowbar, but she's damn good at Southern cooking. My maid Bertha I already talked about. Aside from the gardener that quit, that's all the servants I have."

"The last thing I need to talk to you about is my fee. I charge a hundred dollars a day plus expenses," I said. Virginia just waved her hand away from her body in dismissal, like such trivial amounts were of no consequence. Technically, since I was already theoretically being paid by Tony Cardello, taking a fee from Virginia could be considered unethical. But since I didn't expect to ultimately receive a penny from either of them, I figured I might as well try. Who knew, maybe Virginia and Tony would come through and both pay me. In that case, I would donate the extra fee to a worthy charity, like the Matthew Cole Whiskey Endowment Fund for lame young private eyes.

My experience as a policeman and detective had over the years instilled in me the ability to size up people pretty well. I usually could tell when folks were lying and trying to run a con on me. Using that experience as a guide, I strongly suspected that Virginia Hill, despite her brass and bravado act, was underneath a deeply unhappy woman playing a role she was sick of.

After leaving Virginia Hill's dressing room, Solly escorted me back downstairs. I made my way carefully down the stairs holding onto the handrail.

Captain straight: "Well, so far so good. You didn't get thrown out of any upstairs windows. Now, all we have to do is talk to the servants and then get the hell out of here."

The Brat: "Yeah, we can go back to the office and have a drink. I'm parched."

At the bottom of the steps, I turned right toward the kitchen and almost collided with Benjamin "Bugsy" Siegel, the kingpin of the mob's west coast rackets.

CHAPTER SEVEN

BEVERLY HILLS
JUNE 7, 1947
SATURDAY
1:50 P.M.

Ben Siegel had his suit jacket slung over his left shoulder and was holding on to it with his left hand, because of the warm day I presumed. He was tall, with a body that appeared athletic and powerful and with loads of medium brown wavy hair topping a movie star handsome face. Right then that face was wearing a cross between a smirk and a quizzical expression.

"Who the hell are you?" he asked in a mildly surprised tone.

Before he had got the words completely out of his mouth, one of his bodyguards darted around Siegel, shoved me against a wall and pointed a .38 revolver in my face. The bodyguard was tall and cadaverously thin with an unhealthy, sallow pallor on the skin of his narrow face. He had a long pointed nose that had been broken at some point and not set properly because it veered off to port at the end like a ski jump in need of repair. Smallpox scars pocked the skin of his cheeks. The thug was as ugly as Siegel was handsome. But it was the eyes that I saw behind the sights of the gun that gave me pause. They were murderous and contained not a shred of pity. They made me feel like I had just bumped into the Devil himself in a graveyard on Halloween. I tried to answer Siegel but no words came out when I tried to speak.

"Solly, get your ass over here and tell me who this guy is," called Siegel into the kitchen behind him.

I didn't see Solly approach the knot of men around Siegel. I was too busy looking cross-eyed trying to focus on the muzzle of the gun inches from my nose.

"He's okay boss. He's a private dick. Virginia called him out here to look into her missing bracelet," said Solly.

Siegel must have given Solly a stern look because he immedicably began to whine.

"Do not look at me like that Boss, it was not my idea. She calls dis guy witout tellin' me first. What was I sposed ta do? You know how Virginia is."

Siegel turned back to me. "Okay, Vinnie, put the gun down and let this bird settle down. We wouldn't want him to have a heart attack and die. Then we'd have to dispose of the body," he said, then turned his head to look at me.

"So Virginia hired you to look for her stupid fucking bracelet. Well okay then, look for the fucking bracelet. I would put my money on that broad Carmen Cardello as the thief. I'll make you a deal, when or if you find Carmen let me know where she is and then back off. I got some unfinished business with her. In the meantime, while you're snooping around this house, keep the fuck out of my way," said Siegel.

Ever since that grenade went off on Guadalcanal and scrambled my brains, they don't work quite like other people. In times of great stress, I think of the damnedest things. Right then I was considering whether to tell Siegel that I was going to charge him my usual fee for finding Carmen too. If he were to pay it would amount to several hundred dollars more for the Matthew Cole Whiskey Endowment Fund for lame young private eyes.

Captain Straight: "Don't you dare! This is not the time to get cute."

The brat: "For once I agree with the Captain. Clam the hell up."

Siegel then turned away and walked up the stairs toward Virginia's bedroom. Vinnie the cadaverous bodyguard disappeared toward the front of the house. I let out the breath I had been holding for about a minute and a half.

"Well," I said to nobody in particular, "that was fun."

I limped back into the kitchen. Carlo, the mountain and a half and Solly were not there. They were probably out beating up a neighbor to try out a new pair of brass knuckles or maybe torturing a stray dog they had caught on the back yard or something. But the cook was there. She was a hefty woman in her sixties with enormous sagging breasts that strained against the fabric of her dress. Contrary to the way Virginia described her, the cook didn't have a face that looked like it had been rearranged with a crowbar. Eight or ten hefty smacks with a sap maybe, but not a crowbar. She was standing beside a food preparation table located in the middle of the room that was groaning under the weight of stacks of food. There were enough lamb chops there to feed a rifle platoon of Marines, with enough left over to allow the "chow-hounds" among them to come back for seconds. Beside to meat, there was a large vat of salad and two sacks of potatoes.

"I take it you're Ethel the cook. I'm Matt C…"

"I know who you are," interrupted Ethel, "nothing's a secret around here for long."

"That's a lot of food. That's not all for one meal is it?"

"Yeah, it is. Mr. Siegel and Miss Hill are light eaters, they'll have one chop each. Vinnie, Solly, and Chick will each have two. The rest is for Carlo. You have to fill him up at dinner or he raids the Frigidaire later on in the evening and there's no food left in the house for breakfast."

"I've met Vinnie, Carlo, and Solly, but who is Chick?"

"He's Miss Hill's brother. He's a Marine stationed down a Camp Pendleton. He usually comes here on weekends to see his sister and stays for Saturday night dinner," said Ethel the cook.

"I wanted to ask you about Carmen Cardello. I believe she was staying here?"

"Yes, for a few weeks I think. Poor thing, I felt sorry for her. She was told to stay in her little room over the garage and not to come into the house by Mr. Siegel. I took her meals on a tray. She was such a timid little thing and jumpy as a baby deer. About the only person who ever talked to her was the young man who mowed the lawn. I saw the two of them sitting on the steps that lead up to her room several times. They were talking and I think those are the only times I ever saw Carmen smile. "

This kid that mowed the lawn, do you know his name?" I asked.

Wade Perkins, I think, yes Wade Perkins. He told me once that he lives with his parents in a house near Third and Highland."

"What kind of a guy was he?"

Ethel thought a moment then said: "He was your typical American young man, about twenty or twenty-one, friendly and outgoing. That is until one day last week, I believe it was Monday, he said something to Solly that he didn't like and Solly slapped him. I think that was why he up and quit his job."

"Thanks for your help," I told Ethel the cook and went looking for Solly. I found him sitting in a lawn chair in the backyard smoking a cigar.

"Solly, who was that skinny guy with the pocked face," I asked.

"He's Vinnie Alfonsi, Ben's head bodyguard. I would not mess with him if I was you," said Solly. " Him and Ben go way back to da early New York days."

"Did you slap the kid who used to mow the lawn around here?"

"You're damn right I did. I made a half-assed jokin' comment about Carmen's big tits and the little prick called me a ass-hole. I only slapped him. I should have done to him what somebody probably did to Johnny Falcone."

"Who is Johnny Falcone?" I asked.

"He is Jack Dragna's favorite nephew. He is also a cocky little shit who went missing, and in our line of work if yer missing, dat means yer probly dead and food for the fishies."

Jack Dragna had been the top banana for the Chicago mob in Los Angeles in the late thirties when Siegel, working for "Lucky" Luciano and Meyer Lansky of the New York mob, came to California and muscled in. Siegel took over more than half of Dragna's gambling and prostitution operations. It was rumored that there was still, after all these years, very bad blood between Jack Dragna and Ben Siegel. I personally had some dealings with Jack Dragna's boys in the past. They were people you definitely didn't want mad at you.

"Now gway. Yer botherin' me," said Solly.

"I want to go look at Carmen's room over the garage. Is that okay," I asked.

He didn't answer me verbally, only flipped his hand toward the garage. I interpreted this gesture as permission and limped through the ankle-high grass of the backyard to a flight of rickety wooden stairs leading up to the rooms above the garage.

There turned out to be two small cheaply constructed rooms with a Jack and Jill bathroom connecting them. They were obviously constructed a long time ago by the owner of the mansion as quarters for servants. The first of the two rooms I came to on the wooden walkway was unused, had a bed bare of sheets and smelled like dust. The room was obviously unoccupied. I backed out and went to the door of the second room.

This one was different. Just inside the door, I detected the scent of lilacs, so I knew the room had been recently occupied by a woman. The place was a dump with trash and dirty dishes on a tray sitting on a small two-person Formica table. There were items of various female clothing hanging haphazardly on wire hangers from nails pounded into the plaster walls, and a closed suitcase on a low table at the foot of the unmade bed. A stack of True Romance magazines collected dust on the nightstand by the bed. I opened the lid of the suitcase and saw more female clothing, but these items looked like they had been worn and then wadded up and put away dirty. In the bathroom on a shelf over the sink was an assortment of lotions, curlers, and other woman's beauty junk.

Coming back into the bedroom, my eye detected a green object protruding from under the bed that I hadn't seen before because it had been partially obscured by a blanket. I reached down and retrieved the object. It was a medium-sized woman's green leather purse with a strap handle. Inside was more woman's beauty junk and a tan leather wallet with "CARMEN" embossed on it. There were six bucks in the wallet but no identification.

Captain Straight: "It's obvious that Carmen must have left here in a hell of a hurry if she didn't take her purse or any of her other stuff with her."

The Brat: "Yeah, but did she leave under her own power or was she dragged out? There's no pools of blood or spatter around so she probably wasn't shot or stabbed in here."

Captain Straight: "No signs of a struggle either. She could have been sapped and carried out, but my intuition tells me that she probably saw something happen that scared her so much that she bolted and didn't even come back for her things."

The Brat: "The question then is, did she get clean away or was she caught later on?"

Captain Straight: "If she did get away, where the hell is she?"

I backed out of the room leaving all Carmen's things in place. If this grubby little room turned out to be a crime scene in the future, I didn't want to disturb it any further. I looked down at the alley from the wooden walkway. I saw that the garage had a large sliding door facing the alley. That meant the garage had access doors on both sides. I made my way back down to ground level and walked over to the closed sliding garage door facing the back yard. When I got close I saw that the door was secured with a hefty padlock. The door had a row of tiny windows running horizontally across its top portion. I was standing on my tippy-toes, trying to peer in one of these windows when I heard a shout.

"What the hell are you lookin at? Get the hell away from there!"

I turned toward the voice and saw Vinnie Alfonsi hurrying toward me.

"Get yer ass away from there and go back in the house. If I ever catch you nosin round that garage, I'll ventilate you," said Vinnie, not very gently.

The Brat: " Hmmm, I think there is something in that garage that Vinnie definitely doesn't want anybody to see, right Captain?"

Captain Straight: "Yup."

Solly was still in the same chair and still smoking the same cigar which was now down to a one-inch stub. We didn't speak when I walked by him and approached the kitchen door.

When I limped into the kitchen, I came face to face with a tall, well-built man in his mid-twenties, wearing the tan tropical uniform of a Marine corporal. His face was very ordinary looking and the only distinguishing feature about him was his military, "high and tight" haircut. The corporal gave me a dismissive look, then strolled over to the Frigidaire, opened the door, reached in and a moment later his hand emerged holding a bottle of Schlitz beer. He uncapped it with a church-key he got from a drawer and took a long pull, ignoring me the whole time.

"What outfit are you with?" I asked.

"What's it to ya?" he replied as he shook out a cigarette from a pack of Lucky Strikes and searched his pockets for matches. I ambled over to him with my hand out holding my zippo lighter and fired it up, making sure the Marine emblem riveted to it was visible. The Marine leaned down and lit his cigarette of my lighter. He took a deep drag on the butt then expelled the smoke.

"You an ex-jarhead?" he asked.

"Yeah, served as an infantryman in Puller's battalion of the Seventh Marines on the Canal. It's where I got this," I said and tapped my gimpy left leg. "Got blown up by a Jap grenade."

"Well," the Marine said as he reached to shake my hand, "I was with the Twenty-Ninth Marines on Okinawa. Got through without a scratch. I'm now a mortarman with the 3rd Marine brigade at Pendleton." We shook warmly.

"My name is Charley Hill, but my friends call me 'Chick.' And anyone who served under Chesty Puller on Guadalcanal is a friend of mine."

"Glad to meet you Chick. I'm Matt Cole. I'm a private investigator your sister hired to find her missing bracelet. I presume you know about the missing bracelet."

"Yeah, I know about it. It's a wonder more shit doesn't go missing around this madhouse, with shady people coming and going all the time."

I handed Chick one of my business cards and said: "If you're still in town tomorrow, maybe we could get together and have a few beers. There are some questions I have that maybe you could answer. I'll buy the beer, wine or whiskey, whatever you prefer."

"Sure chum, I'll call you tomorrow about one in the afternoon," replied Chick and walked out of the kitchen toward the front of the house.

My interview with Bertha, Virginia's maid wasn't very productive. The sullen woman declared that she had never touched Virginia's jewelry box in the many years she had been in her employ. Aside from that, she didn't know nothing from nothing and even if she did she wouldn't tell me.

With much relief, I limped past Carlo the mountain and a half and out the front door of Virginia's mansion about three o'clock in the afternoon. To walk out of that place under my own power made me feel like Superman did that time he buried Lex Luthor deep under the ruins of the Empire State building. But The Brat and I were in dire need of a drink. I high tailed it to my apartment. I would have gone to my office but because it was after noon, it was closed. I parked my car in my private space back of my apartment building and then made my way to a little neighborhood bar about a block away. The bar was a dive. It wasn't friendly or in any other way appealing. I chose it for its proximity to where I slept. That way when I emerged in several hours soused to the gills, I wouldn't have to worry about getting a 502 on the way home.

CHAPTER EIGHT

LOS ANGELES
JUNE 8, 1947
SUNDAY
9:30 A.M.

I woke up with my usual Sunday morning hangover. From experience, I knew the only cure was a big breakfast, gallons of coffee, and most importantly, a little hair of the dog. I selected a glass from the dirty ones in the sink, cleaned it using my patented thumb technique, and made myself a Bloody Mary, then tossed it down. It tasted so good, I made another. Feeling a little better, I shaved while smoking a butt, maneuvering the razor around the lit cigarette and dressed in a lightweight tropical suit.

I drove to my favorite breakfast place, Nick's Café on Spring Street. Since it was only about ten in the morning, the place wasn't busy yet and wouldn't be until the churches let out around noon. Rosita the waitress brought me bacon and three eggs over medium, hash browns and a stack of six big buttermilk pancakes

that I drenched in butter and maple syrup. As I ate, I read a copy
of the Los Angeles Times just to keep up on current events.

The Brat liked the comic pages so I read them first. It was
amusing to me to hear him laugh at the lame and silly jokes of the
cartoon characters. His favorites were the Katzenjammer Kids
and Lil' Abner. Next, I skimmed through the sports pages. It was
baseball season but I had never been a fan of baseball. Maybe it
was because all the major league games were played in the eastern
half of the country and I didn't identify with any of them.

The front page of the Times printed a speech by President
Truman wherein he blasted the Republicans congress as "Do
nothings." I was no fan of the Republicans but I detested Truman.
To me, he was just a loud-mouthed little asshole that wanted to
do away with the Marine Corps and shift the personnel to the
army. Being a former Marine this didn't sit well with me. The rest
of the front section was given over to coverage of the guerilla war
being fought between the Arabs and the Jews in Palestine, with
the British caught in the middle, and the Indian war for
independence from the same British. I thought that maybe it was
time for the British to get it into their heads that they couldn't
haughtily rule over all the little brown and black people anymore.
Those days were over.

When I looked at the back page of the main section of the
Times, I was confronted by a picture of Bugsy Siegel, elegantly
dressed with a good looking blonde starlet draped over his arm.

Underneath the picture was the headline: "Is a gang war about to break out in Los Angeles?" Below the headline was the story:

Los Angeles, June 8, 1947
Story by Times staff reporter Pete Barnes

Tensions between the Chicago and New York factions of the Los Angeles underworld seemed to be rising toward the boiling point Saturday. A reliable source has told the Times that since the disappearance of Johnny Falcone, 22, nephew of Jack Dragna, who is believed to be affiliated with the Chicago underworld faction, anger and distrust have arisen between the underworld groups. Individuals within Dragna's circle tell the Times that they believe that reputed New York affiliated gangster Benjamin Siegel, Playboy, and friend to Hollywood stars, is responsible for Falcone's disappearance. Whether the tension will erupt in open warfare on our Los Angeles streets is anyone's guess.

The Brat: "Way to go slick. You get yourself hired by Bugsy Siegel's girlfriend just as a gang war is about to kick off. Do you have any more bright ideas? Like maybe parachuting into Moscow to assassinate Stalin?"

Captain Straight: "It wasn't Matt's fault and you know it. Think about it. Carlo was the one who opened his yap about Matt being so good at finding things."

The Brat: "I'm just saying that our boy has a shitty sense of timing."

I finished breakfast and reading the Times at about the same time, eleven o'clock. Then I drove back to my office. I settled myself in my office chair to await Chick's call.

The Brat: "Who're you kidding, that Marine isn't going to call. You're wasting your time."

Captain Straight: "How the hell do you know, maybe he will."

The Brat: "Oh maybe this and maybe that. How come you're so damn optimistic all the time? Maybe if Bing Crosby was born without balls they'd call him Betty Crocker."

"SHUT UP!" I yelled out loud. "Can't you two bastards stifle it for just a little while?"

I opened my center drawer and got out my chart showing the different time zones around the world. Using the chart I calculated that it was five-fifteen P.M. in Stockholm, Sweden. I took out an unopened bottle of Jack Daniel's Old No.7 Whiskey, broke the seal and uncorked it. Next, I took out my glass and filled it with whiskey to the very top. I held up the glass.

"Skoal," I said to the empty room.

Chick called at ten after one. He called the public number printed on my card and not my private number handwritten on the back. I heard the phone ring out at Betty's counter in the reception area. I hurried out there but the phone had rung about seven times before I finally figured out Betty's PBX gadget and plugged the right cord into the right hole.

"Hey Matt, you still want to ask me some questions? I got about an hour or two to kill before I got to get back to the base."

We arranged to meet at the King Eddy Saloon at 5th and Los Angeles streets, my favorite downtown bar. The bar had been there since 1906. When I walked into the place I savored the pleasing aroma of decades of spilled beer mingled with old sweat and the unique sharper tang of thousands of ancient cigars smoked by long-dead men wearing derby hats. The place was dark inside, just the way I liked it, with smoke-stained wood paneling on the walls and ceiling. Three regulars sat hunched over their drinks at the long mahogany bar. I saw Chick sitting at a table in the back. I joined him.

"Boy you sure picked a good time to leave Jenny's house yesterday," said Chick as I sat down and signaled the bartender to come over and take our order. "An hour after you left, Mickey Cohen showed up with six hard guys toting more ordinance than a panzer division on the march. Cohen had a conference with Siegel and then stationed guards all around the perimeter of the house. Everybody including Ben Siegel looked all white and strained like they were constipated and hadn't shit for a week. You have any idea what it's all about?"

"Yeah, there was an article in the paper predicting a gang war between Siegel's guys and Jack Dragna's guys. It seems a gent named, Johnny Falcone, Dragna's nephew, has disappeared and Dragna thinks Siegel rubbed him out."

"Well, no wonder everyone at the house was so jumpy. I guess it would be going way too far for me to ask God to give Ben Siegel his comeuppance this time."

"You don't like Siegel?" I asked.

"I hate his fuckin' guts, but don't you tell him I said that. If he knew how I felt, the bastard's goons wouldn't let me see my sister. I'm trusting you as a fellow combat veteran not to rat on me."

" Hey, man, your secret's safe with me. I haven't got any special regard for Bugsy either. But why do you hate him so much?"

"He's worked over Jenny more than a few times during arguments. He's careful to hit her where the bruises won't show and acts sorry afterward. But he's not sorry. The son of a bitch just gets his jollies beating up women and I've decided that if he does it again, it'll be his last time," said Chick menacingly and without a smile. I didn't believe he was kidding.

The bartender came over and we ordered our drinks. Bourbon neat for me and a tall beer for Chick. We didn't speak again until the barman set our drinks in front of us and retreated.

"Why doesn't Virginia just get out of there?"

"It's a little complicated and will take a little time to explain, but here goes," said the Marine.

"Jenny and I were born in a one-horse shithole of a town in Alabama. There were ten kids in the family in all with Jenny being the oldest. Our old man was a drunk who couldn't keep a job and spent money the family needed for food on hooch. Not only that, he would come home drunk as a skunk and beat on the kids and my ma. The older kids were forced to go out and beg or steal so the littler kids wouldn't starve."

"By the time Jenny was in her late teens, she had had enough and ran away. She ended up in Chicago and worked first as a waitress, then as a party girl for the mob. Chicago was under the control of Al Capone at that time and my sister worked her way up into being a money courier for the Chicago mob. She met a mob-connected guy named Joey Epstein who made her his protégé."

Chick paused and looked at me with sad eyes. "Jenny did some things then that people condemn her for now. But she only did them to survive. She was a young woman alone in a big city living by her wits and she had to do what she had to do."

I nodded to him but made no comment.

"In 1937 while in New York on mob business, she met Ben Siegel. They were instantly in lust for each other and embarked on an on-again, off-again love affair. Jenny thought she loved him for a while until he started slapping her around, and she broke it off, she thought, for good."

"In 1938 Lucky Luciano and Meyer Lansky of the New York mob sent Ben Siegel and Mickey Cohen to Los Angeles. The excuse given to Jack Dragna, who at that time controlled the west coast rackets for the Chicago mob, was that Siegel was there to set up an organization controlled wire service to report race results from western tracks to betting parlors in the east. Well, it wasn't long before Siegel and Cohen started to muscle in on Dragna and take over more than half the Chicago mob's betting parlors and whore houses in Los Angeles. The Chicago boys didn't like it, but weren't powerful enough to resist."

"My sister was working for Joey Epstein in Chicago at the time. Charlie Fischetti, Al Capone's cousin and political fixer for the Chicago mob, called Jenny in. He ordered her to go to L.A. and restart her affair with Siegel. If she could do it, Fischetti said she was to report back to him everything that Siegel did. Jenny didn't want to go, but how do you say no to a guy with a mob nickname of "trigger happy." Ever since Jenny has been regularly sending messages about Ben's activities to Fischetti through Jack Dragna. Siegel thinks every woman is in love with him including my sister. But she can't stand the son of a bitch."

By that time both of us had drained our drinks and I signaled to the bartender for another round. After they were served, Chick Hill resumed his narrative.

"The Hollywood nitwits he hangs around with think Ben Siegel is this handsome, romantic, tough but actually harmless guy they met at a cocktail party at George Raft's house. But let me tell you about the real Ben Siegel that my sister told me about."

"In the early thirties, Al Anastasia and Louis Buchalter formed Murder Incorporated in New York. It was a murder for hire outfit and was the enforcement arm for the New York crime families. Altogether there were thousands of guys rubbed out by them. Ben Siegel was their chief killer. He was so ruthless and efficient that he was promoted to be chief lieutenant to Al Anastasia himself. He became tight with Lucky Luciano and palled around with Meyer Lansky, who he had known as a young boy. But Ben had a problem. He loved killing so much that he went overboard carrying out his hits. Instead of just shooting a guy in the back of the head, Ben would beat a guy with a baseball bat until you couldn't recognize him as human. Siegel's brutality began to become a problem for the mob in the late thirties. The public was turning against the gangsters because they were tired of all the messy killings. Luciano decided to get Siegel out of town, so he sent him to L.A. with orders to try and get along with Jack Dragna and play nice."

"They don't call Ben Siegel "Bugsy" for nothing. The guy has a screw loose. He can go from talking to a guy in a friendly tone, to a rage where he's beating the guy to a pulp in one second flat. Once he gets started on one of his rages, he can't control himself."

"But Siegel may be in for more trouble than he can handle. My sister told me that at an organization get together in Havana a few months ago, Meyer Lansky and Lucky Luciano were openly saying that they suspected Siegel of skimming money from the construction budget of the new Flamingo Hotel in Las Vegas. The place cost six million to build and Lansky figured it shouldn't have cost over four. If this is true, you can imagine what will happen to a guy that steals from Lucky Luciano."

"I don't know why I told you all this stuff. If you were to blab, it could cause a lot of trouble for Jenny and probably get me killed. But I needed to talk to somebody. And if you can't trust a Jarhead who fought and was wounded under Chesty Puller on Guadalcanal, who can you trust?"

'Don't worry. I have no inclination or reason to talk to Siegel ever again. I'm just trying to find a missing girl," I said as I took Carmen Cardello's picture from my wallet and showed it to Chick.

"Did you ever see this girl at Virginia's house?"

Chick squinted at the picture and then shook his head. "Nope never saw her," he replied.

Hill got up from his chair. "Well, I gotta go catch the bus for Pendleton. See ya around. I hope I was some help?"

REQUIEM FOR BUGSY | 97

"Thanks, buddy, you were a ton of help. If I can ever return the favor, call me, here's another of my business cards. My home number is written on the back," I said as I handed it over.

After leaving the bar I went home. I cooked myself a dinner of canned chili con carne using a freshly washed pot, bowl, and spoon, according to my system. Afterward, I sipped bourbon, chain-smoked Camel cigarettes and listened to "The Official Detective" program on the radio. I must admit that I didn't hear much of the program. Captain Straight and The Brat were arguing for two hours in my head about which variety of avocados were better tasting, Haas, Gwen or Pinkerton. I was asleep by Ten.

CHAPTER NINE

LOS ANGELES
JUNE 9, 1947
MONDAY
9:00 A.M.

I limped from the elevator to the reception area of my office only a little hungover. I was angered to see the man who had donated sperm to my mother allowing me to be conceived, sitting in the reception area and looking at me expectantly. I ignored him and continued on to Betty's counter. She looked different. She had a new hairstyle, was wearing red lipstick and was not as nervous as usual. Maybe she had a new boyfriend and was releasing all that built-up tension by some strenuous after-hours activities, like hot unbridled sex, or maybe tennis.

"Good morning Betty. Any new interoffice memos I should know about?" I asked.

"No, sir, none since Friday morning. Listen, your father waited all Friday afternoon to see you. Now he's back again. Won't you talk to him?"

"Let the son of a bitch wait," I replied and limped to my private office. Once inside I hadn't had time to throw my hat on the window sill, drape my suit jacket on the back of my chair and light up a Camel cigarette before Mrs. Adderley strolled in holding a stack of magazines, followed by her ever-present assistant, Luann. Luann looked particularly stressed that day, both of her eyes were alternately twitching so prominently that she looked like one of those poles with blinking lights at a railroad crossing.

"Mr. Cole, I just came in to offer my assistance on the secret project you are working on. Maybe I can help you with research or something."

"Oh, no," I declared. "Loose lips sink ships."

"I beg your pardon?"

"Mrs. Adderley, if I told you about what I've been working on and you blabbed, whole intelligence networks would be compromised and a bunch of innocent Russians would be rounded up and shot. In fact, as Harry Truman was pouring me a glass of bourbon after giving me this assignment, he said to me, 'Matt, whatever you do, don't tell that Adderley woman in your office about this. We got a file on her. We think her real name is

Olga Smirnov and we think she's an NKVD agent.' And don't try looking through my desk after I'm gone looking for clues to what I'm doing either, because there's nothing here. And if you think you can sneak a swig on my bourbon bottle while you're rifling through my drawers, think again. I have the level on the bottle marked. And finally, don't try the old trick of guzzling half the bottle and replacing it with water. I can tell by the color of the booze if you try to do that."

"Are you through?" said Mrs. Adderley, pinning me with a stare that old Uncle Joe Stalin would display as he's happily sending half of Romania off to labor camps in Siberia. Hell, maybe Mrs. Adderley really was an NKVD mole!

"Yes, that's all I have to say for now."

"Good," she said and laid the stack of magazines on top of my desk. "You threw such a childish tantrum about not being notified beforehand about our last advertising campaign, I have decided to run phase two by you and get your input. We plan to advertise in at least two of these national magazines."

I picked up the top two magazines on the stack. The first was "Modern Romance." I could see the logic of putting an ad in it. The second magazine was called, "Hollywood Undercover." I leafed through it. About halfway through I came across a large color photograph of Bugsy Siegel. He was coming out of a restaurant dressed to the nines with a good looking blonde starlet on his arm. I flipped it closed and was about to return it to the stack when The Brat spoke up.

"Wait a minute! Go back and look at that picture of Bugsy. Look at the babe's wrist."

I retrieved the magazine and checked the date of issue. It was two days ago. I found the picture of Siegel again and looked closely at the wrist of his blonde companion. She was wearing a bracelet with four rows of sparkling stones interrupted in the center by a diamond-shaped pattern of red jewels!

"Mrs. Adderley," I exclaimed, " Buy everybody in the place lunch on me!" I got up from my desk and rushed out past my astonished office manager and out to where my car was parked. I drove the most direct route to Virginia Hill's house in Beverly Hills.

The door was opened by Bertha the maid and she didn't look any more pleasant than the last time. In fact, this time she was ruder. She was giving me an evil stare that reminded me of Doctor Destructo's x-ray death beam. Once inside the door, Carlo the mountain and a half came up to me. I looked around because Siegel spent his weekdays in Las Vegas, all the extra guards had gone too.

"I need to see Virginia right away," I told the mountain and a half.

"Okay, Peeper, wait in the kitchen."

I limped down the hallway and seated myself at the kitchen table with the magazine on the table in front of me. After about five minutes, Virginia came in wearing a dark blue dress, a round hat, elbow-length kid gloves and carrying a purse. It looked like she had been preparing to go out when I came. She looked at me expectantly.

"I found out where your bracelet is, but I have no way of recovering it. You'll have to arrange to do that yourself," I said and handed over the magazine opened to the picture of Siegel and the blonde.

Virginia looked at the photograph in the magazine with a puzzled expression for a few moments, then I saw her face harden and go red with anger.

"That rotten son of a bitch!" she spat out. "I'll kill that bastard."

"Well, I guess that concludes our arrangement. Good luck in the future. I kind of like you, which I can't say about most of my clients," I said and started to turn away to leave.

"Just a minute," she said and opened her purse. She reached inside and her hand came out holding three C-notes. "This is for you."

I took the money without further comment, went out to my car and drove away.

When I limped back into the reception area of my office, my biological sire (I refused to refer to him as my father) was still there and stood up from one of the rock hard couches.

'Please Matthew, we have to talk. It'll only take a few minutes of your time," he said in a pleading voice.

I stopped, took a deep breath and then expelled it. "Alright, if that's the only way to get rid of you, c'mon," I said.

He followed me to my private office where we sat down across from each other with my desk between us. "Okay, say what you have to say," I said none too gently.

"Matthew, I know you hate me so I will make this as short as possible. But I owe it to you to tell you the truth about how your mother and I split up."

"If you're going to try to tell me it was my mother's fault, you can just get the hell out of here right now. Next, you'll be telling me that it wasn't cruel to abandon a six-year-old boy who loved you. Do you know that for years I blamed myself for your leaving? I thought I had done something bad to make you go away. Then I finally came to realize that you were just no good and not worth thinking about anymore," I said.

"Matthew I've lived for almost sixty years now. When you get to my age you will realize that people are seldom as saintly, or as evil as they are portrayed to be by others. In 1920 there was a terrible financial panic in America. Businesses were shuttered and plants closed. I lost my job at the Goodyear plant. The economic hard times went on and on. I couldn't find steady work to support you and your mother. By 1922, we were just eking out a living. I worked odd jobs or anything I could get to earn a few dollars. Your mother helped out by working as a waitress during the day for tips."

"Then one day while you were at school, the tension boiled over and we had a big fight. Your mother told me she was tired of living with a bum like me and told me to get out. I said some pretty terrible things too. I packed my cardboard suitcase and left. I wasn't thinking about anything except the hurt and anger. That night I hopped a freight train headed north. By the time I reached Fresno, my anger had dissipated and all that was left was the hurt. I missed you and your mother already. I caught a train going back south and showed up at home the next day. I begged your mother for forgiveness, but she told me she didn't want anything more to do with me. I pleaded with her but she wouldn't relent. I told her I wanted to say goodbye to you but she said no, that it would be too hard on you. Then I left for good. When my business in Seattle started to be profitable, I sent your mother monthly checks. Sometimes she cashed the checks, sometimes not. But I never stopped thinking about you and wondering how you were doing. I kept tabs on you secretly through the years and when I learned that you had become a Marine, I was so proud I thought I would burst."

"Okay, so that's supposed to make it alright? You still deserted me. Why didn't you write to me and tell me you still loved me?"

"I did write to you, many times in the early years, but all my letters came back marked, 'Return to sender,' or didn't come back at all."

What he said stirred a memory in me. I was about eight or nine and one day I saw my mother burning an unopened letter on the kitchen stove. I asked her why she was burning the mail without reading it first. She snapped at me and said that it was none of my business.

"Have you ever heard of 'Old King Cole's Spicy English Mustard'?" my sire asked.

"Sure, everybody has. I like it on my hotdogs. Every diner I know has it, if not on the tables, at least available upon request."

"Well, until two weeks ago, I was Old King Cole's Spicy English Mustard. I owned the company outright as well as five smaller companies. The reason I have traveled all this way is to tell you that my doctors have informed me that I have inoperable lung cancer and I will die quite soon, in four to six months if I'm lucky."

"After I moved to Seattle I met a woman named Florence. She has been my life's companion and I love her dearly. I have arranged for her to be taken care of financially for the rest of her life. We never had any children. The bulk of my estate will go to you Matthew, you are my only heir."

As my Father got up to go, he reached into his briefcase and took a three-inch stack of what looked like old letters from it. The letters were held together by a black ribbon tied in a bow. He handed them to me.

"I am staying at the Hollywood Roosevelt Hotel for a few more days. If you feel the need to talk more or have any questions, come and see me," my father said and left quietly.

After he left I poured a stiff drink and tossed it down. I didn't know what to think. I untied the black ribbon and examined the unopened letters. Each one was addressed to Matt Cole at various addresses where my mom and I had lived during the twenties and early thirties. On each letter, there was a scrawl that I identified as my mother's lousy handwriting stating: "Return to sender." I picked one at random and opened it.

Oct. 15, 1930

Dear Matt.

How are you? Are you doing well in school? I wish you would write to me and tell me about your life. Hey, I've got an idea. Why don't you visit me in Seattle? We could have a lot of fun. The fishing is great here. Think about it and ask your mother. Thinking of you constantly.

Love, Dad.

I selected another letter at random and opened it.

January 21, 1927

Dear Matt:

I hope you are feeling well. I think about you all the time. I know that you are angry with me and wouldn't want to see me. But I miss you so much. If you get this letter, please write to me. You don't have to tell your mother that you did. It will be our secret.

Your loving father.

Tears welled up in my eyes and ran down my cheeks. But having spent years hating the man, it wasn't possible for me to just turn on a dime and start loving him again. To tell the truth I was angry at my father not just for the hurt he had caused to me and my mother, but also for having to grow up without a father. I remembered incidences when I was young when other boys my age were bragging about their dads taking them hunting, fishing, to a ball game or some other fun activity. I was so envious at those times that I often belittled the other boys' closeness with their dads and it sometimes led to fistfights. Because he had been gone, I had no memories of doing things with my father after age six and I deeply resented him for it.

Despite all I had learned that day, it would have been easy to continue hating my father, but other inconvenient memories started to intrude on my thoughts. I had grown up idolizing my mother. With me, she could do no wrong. But what my dad had just told me and reading the letters my mother refused to give me, had caused me to reluctantly reexamine my mother's personality and her quirks. She had been a black and white kind of person. Something was either right or wrong, with no gray areas in between. If she soured on a person, that was it, she didn't want to have anything more to do with him or her. Except for my petty indiscretions, the word forgiveness wasn't in her lexicon. My mother had very few friends. Looking back with this fresh perspective I could see now that she had been a bitter, unhappy woman, only caring for one person in her life and that was me.

Did that absolve my father of all responsibility for the broken home I grew up in? Probably not. I'm sure he contributed to the breakup and deserved some of the blame and I didn't feel I was ready to commit to forgiving him yet. Throughout the conversation with my dad and my mental retrospection afterward, the voices in my head had remained quiet, out of respect I guess. But they couldn't remain silent very long. It wasn't in their nature and they began to comment.

Captain Straight: "Maybe you've been too hard on your father all along. People aren't perfect and make God-awful mistakes but it isn't fair to punish them forever for shit they did way in the past."

The Brat: "I say give the old guy a chance. Even though you're trying hard to deny it, you love him. He's your dad."

§

The Hollywood Roosevelt Hotel on Hollywood Boulevard was built in 1926 by a consortium that included Douglas Fairbanks Jr., Mary Pickford, Louis B. Mayer, and Sid Grauman. No other hotel in Los Angeles came near to its opulence, or the prices charged to stay there. Movie stars, prominent politicians and other famous people could regularly be seen hobnobbing in the Hollywood Roosevelt lobby under its intricately carved and painted coffered ceiling. It was arguably the finest hotel in Los Angeles.

I parked in the visitor's lot and approached the huge front entrance. I hadn't meant to be here at all. I left my office intending to go by Billie's house and see if she wanted to go out to grab a bite. But my stupid car came to the hotel instead. I was totally unaware of the opulence of the lobby around me as I limped across the carpeted floor and inquired of the desk clerk the number of my father's room.

"Mr. Cole is in room seven-twenty. Do you wish me to call him and notify him that you are on your way up?" the clerk asked.

"That won't be necessary, I'm his son," I replied and headed toward the elevators.

Captain Straight: " Wow, what a place. I'm surprised your dad would spend this much money on a hotel room."

The Brat: "Why the hell not. He apparently has some bucks. Where do you expect him to stay? A merchant sailor's dive in San Pedro?"

Once on the seventh floor, I approached my destination with trepidation. My palms were sweating and my heart raced as I knocked on my father's hotel room door. He answered the door in his shirt-sleeves with his waistcoat unbuttoned, and holding a newspaper in his left hand. When he recognized me standing there, he smiled, but a very tentative one.

"I was wondering if we could have dinner together and talk," I asked shakily.

"I'd like that very much," he replied softly.

Suddenly, I saw a tear trickle down his cheek. Without my willing them, my legs brought me closer to him. I reached out and took his slight body into my arms, put my head on his shoulder and started to cry. I felt his arms encircled me also.

That's right, cynical tough-guy private eye Matt Cole cried like a baby on his father's shoulder. Tears gushed from my eyes in a torrent. But those cleansing tears contained more than warm, salty water. They also washed away the burden of twenty-four years of hurt, pain, resentment, hate, and sorrow, leaving me feeling clean and new and almost like I had just been reborn. I had my dad back! I don't know how long we stood there but when we finally broke that embrace, I knew we were once again father and son and nothing short of death would ever separate us again.

CHAPTER TEN

LOS ANGELES
JUNE 10, 1947
TUESDAY
10:30 A.M.

I studied the house as I walked up the narrow concrete walkway toward the front door. It was a typical California bungalow probably built between 1900 and 1920. They were usually pretty small with a living room, kitchen, bathroom, and two small bedrooms. This one had no peeling paint on its façade and the front yard wasn't overgrown, but it wasn't meticulously maintained either. It looked as if the resident performed the minimum maintenance necessary to keep his neighbors from yelling at him. The front door was standing open, with a wooden screen door protecting the interior of the house from flying insects as the only barrier. I knocked sharply on the slat portion of the screen door.

A chubby guy in his early forties came to the door and he wasn't happy.

"I'm sorry pal but it's just your bad luck that my wife isn't here right now. She's a sucker for you people. We got a new vacuum cleaner and a bunch of other stuff we don't need. But that's okay when we're forced to move out a here cause we can't pay the rent, we'll have the finest Fuller brush collection in the poorhouse."

"Hold on, mister," I said holding my palms up in a surrender gesture. "I'm not a salesman, I'm a private detective and I need to know if you know of a family living in the neighborhood by the name of Perkins who has a twenty-year-old son named Wade."

"Sorry pal, never heard a them."

I was searching for Wade Perkins because he was the only clue I had that might lead to finding out the whereabouts of Tony Cardello's missing sister, Carmen. Agnes, the cook at Virginia Hill's mansion had said she had seen Carmen and Wade Perkins talking together and smiling. Add to that, Wade had defended Carmen's honor to Solly the gangster guard and got slapped for his trouble. I knew it was a pretty thin lead, but I had a nagging suspicion that if I succeeded in locating Wade Perkins, I would find Carmen too.

I was doing a grid search of the homes in the area around Highland Avenue and Third Street. After canvassing a block of homes, I carefully marked it off on a map I carried in my pocket. What I was doing was good, old fashioned shoe-leather detective work. But it was a pain in the ass and I was forced to do it because every other method I had tried to find Wade Perkins's family home had failed.

Earlier in the morning, I had checked our office copy of the Los Angeles City Directory. This private publication claimed to document the names and addresses of everyone living in Los Angeles. I struck out. There were no families named Perkins listed in their pages living anywhere close to Third and Highland.

Then I drove to the high school nearest the intersection and checked out their yearbooks from two to four years in the past. The only kid named Perkins I saw listed was Black. Next, I checked with Water and power, Ma Bell and the gas company and still came up empty. So I was left with finding the Perkins family on foot. It was boring, mindless work, but it gave me plenty of time to reflect on my newfound relationship with my father.

§

The two of us talked for two hours over dinner the night before in the hotel dining room. And then in the bar until two in the morning when we were kicked out. It may sound like a long conversation, but twenty-four years was a long time to catch up on.

I started out by telling my father, in as much detail as I could remember, the story of my life from the time he left to the other day when he walked into my hostile reception at my detective agency. When I got to the part about how I was wounded that hellish night on Guadalcanal when I had hundreds of yelling, Japanese charging at me, his face turned somber and his knuckles turned white as he gripped the arms of his chair. I even told my father about the voices in my head, something I had kept from everyone else in my life. He didn't react like I thought he would. He only smiled and nodded.

It may sound silly, but I interpreted my father's reaction to my telling him about Little Matt, Captain Straight, and The Brat as confirmation that he really loved me and wasn't just running a scam on me. What I told him, as goofy as I sounded, didn't matter because he really loved me. Conversely, if I told anyone else in my life about my voices, I would end up in a straightjacket with a guy dressed in white asking me why I divided my forces just before the battle of Waterloo and sent half the French army off chasing the Prussians.

Then it was my dad's turn to talk. I must admit that by that time both he and I were pretty snockered and my memories of what he said are hazy, to say the least. The gist of it was that he was working in Seattle when a fellow worker bragged about a recipe for mustard that had been handed down in his family for generations. When my father tried it, he liked it so much that he proposed that the two of them become partners and manufacture the stuff. My dad put up all the money he had saved for two years.

Against all expectations, the spicy mustard was a hit with the people of Seattle. Then his partner died of a heart attack. The man's family wanted to sell the business, so my father borrowed money from a bank and bought them out, becoming sole owner. Over the intervening years, the business grew and grew, and my father became more and more prosperous. When my father finished telling his story, it was a quarter to two and a lull settled over us, we were all talked out. I broke the silence with a question.

"What kind of cancer do you have, and are the doctors sure it's so bad you're going to die?"

"Unfortunately it's a terminal disease. I already got a second and third opinion. It started in the prostate gland and over time spread to my other organs. Nope, all I can look forward to is another three to four months. The doctors tell me there will be a lot of pain toward the end and I will have to take increasing amounts of drugs. You can understand now why I came down here at this time. I had to tell you about your inheritance."

"You keep talking about my inheritance. All it does is make me sad by reminding me that after finding you after all these years, that I'm going to be forced to give you up again. How much money are we talking about anyway," I asked, expecting it would be maybe ten thousand or so.

"A little over two million dollars."

Captain Straight: "Huh?"

The Brat: "Holy Shit!"

I was stunned. I sat back in my chair in the quiet bar and was silent for a while.

The Brat: "I think you should keep quiet about this. Don't tell anybody, especially your girlfriend Billie. If she gets wind of this she'll knock you out with a sap and you'll wake up propped up at the altar with the minister asking if you heard his last question, you know the one, 'Do you take this woman?' Her dad will also be there with a shotgun. Not to point at you, but to keep at bay the two thousand or so other gold-digging babes trying to break down the church door and tie the knot with you."

Captain Straight: "It should be good news, but the fact your father has to die for you to benefit kind of puts a damper on things."

The Brat: "In fact, we don't need Billie anymore. Do you know that long sexual dry spell you've been complaining about? Well, I can confidently predict that it'll be over very soon. Once the news of this get's out, that muted thud you'll hear will be the collective sound of thousands of pairs of panties all hitting the floor at the same time. You'll be amazed at how much more handsome and attractive you'll suddenly become when the babes find out you have two million dollars in the bank."

I told my dad what The Brat had just said in my head, and the two of us had a good laugh. Before we parted, I arranged to have dinner with him again the next evening.

§

By three P.M. I was tired of going house to house and decided to call it a day. My bad leg was aching and tingling and my feet felt like Tom the Cat's paws after Jerry the Mouse dropped a hod full of bricks on them from the top of Butch's house. I limped back to my car and drove back to my office. When I walked into the reception area, Betty stopped me.

"Mr. Cole, these people have been waiting to see you."

There were three people who had stood up when I entered the room. The first was a tall skinny guy with glasses, wearing a brown suit with a clerical collar. He was past sixty with a narrow pinched face. The second guy was a Catholic priest, also over sixty but chubbier than his companion. The third person was a woman, severely dressed in a woman's suit that buttoned all the way up to her chin. She was the youngster of the group, only about fifty-five, with a severe expression and pursed lips. I walked over to the group.

The Brat: "I bet that old broad hasn't smiled since the McKinley administration."

"Yes, I am Matt Cole. You asked to speak to me?"

The tall, skinny guy in the clerical collar spoke first.

"Yes, Mr. Cole. I am Reverend Miller. May I introduce Father Martin and Miss Alcott." Both nodded at me. "We represent the Greater Los Angeles Decency league. We wish to speak to you regarding your billboards." They didn't extend their hands to shake, so I didn't either.

"Yes, well, if you'll follow me to my private office we will discuss this," I said and ushered them away. Once seated in my office, Reverend miller led off again.

"Mr. Cole, we of the league feel your billboards are a trifle too racy for the eyes of the public. They are suggestive of marital infidelity which is a forbidden subject in polite society. We think they might instill in the minds of vulnerable, weak people the idea that they could consider violating their marriage vows because other people might be doing it."

Miss Alcott then put in her two cents, "Mr. Cole, the billboards in question are also suggestive of illicit, un, ah, sex." She uttered the word like she was spitting out a prune pit that had got stuck in her throat. "The public's vulnerable minds shouldn't be reminded of this subject."

The Brat: "I'll bet her lady parts are dryer than the Kalahari Desert in August."

I pushed my chair back, slapped my thighs and stood. "Well, Reverend Miller, Father Martin and Miss Alcott, I feel the same way you do about those billboards. And let me assure you that they were erected without my consent. If you will follow me I will take you to the person responsible for this whole debacle," I said.

I led the delegation to Mrs. Adderley's closed office door. Swinging open the door without knocking, I saw Mrs. Adderley and Luann sitting on chairs pulled up to a little table. They were enjoying their afternoon tea. I led the delegation into the office. Mrs. Adderley looked at me with mild shock mingled with curiosity. Luann's eye twitches increased from first to third gear, totally skipping over second. I shot my right arm out and pointed my index finger at Mrs. Adderley.

"There, Reverend Miller, Father Martin, and Miss Alcott is the person responsible for corrupting the morals of the entire city of Los Angeles and possibly starting an epidemic of marital infidelity and sin that could ultimately lead to the breakdown of decent human society," I said accusingly.

Mrs. Adderley gaped at me with her mouth open, for once at a loss for words. Luann uttered a little strangling noise from deep in her throat and started levitating upwards off the seat of her chair. I figured if someone didn't grab her arm pretty quick she would bang her head against the ceiling and hurt herself. Now, I must reluctantly admit here that I didn't actually see Luann actually levitate off her chair, but I was sure she was about to.

"Well, I'll leave you all to discuss this little matter. I have an appointment, " I said brightly and left Mrs. Adderley's office.

That night while I was at dinner with my father, he told me that he had been informed by his lawyer about some snags encountered in settling his personal affairs. It was imperative that he return to Seattle as soon as possible. He said he was departing on the first leg of his journey on The Lark, an all-sleeper overnight train to San Francisco, leaving at 9 P.M. from Union Station. We talked for the rest of the evening, I drove him to the station and walked him to the departure gate.

"Matthew, please take some time off and come to Seattle after you finish the big case you're working on. You can say at my home. I want you to meet Florence. I think you two will hit it off nicely. She's sassy just like you. When you come, maybe we can do some of those father-son things we missed out on the past twenty-four years. Oh, and son, how is your business doing? I can wire a hundred thousand or so to your bank if you need it."

"Nah, dad, my finances are all in the black for the time being. I'll see you in Seattle," I said choking back tears. We embraced, and then he was gone.

CHAPTER ELEVEN

LOS ANGELES
JUNE 11, 1947
WEDNESDAY
10:00 A.M.

When I came into the office, Betty flagged me down, " Mr. Cole I have a message here from a Corporal Charles Hill, at the Camp Pendleton Marine Base. He wants you to call him right away. He says it's urgent."

I took the message slip from her hand and walked toward my private office. On the way, I encountered Mrs. Adderley, who gave me the stink eye and walked right past me without speaking. I guessed that she was still pissed at me for my little ambush of the previous day. I couldn't help but wonder how she had handled the complaint from the Greater Los Angeles Decency League.

The Brat: "You better be careful. Check for rattlesnakes in your desk drawers, Black Widow spiders in the cigarette box, acid in your water jug and tripwires attached to grenades with loosened pins in your private john."

Once in my office, I picked up my private phone that wasn't connected to Betty's PBX and dialed "O" to get the operator. When she came on the line I asked for the long-distance operator. There were a series of clicks and a tinny female voice said, "Long-distance" in the peculiar lilt that phone operators used. I placed a person to person, long-distance call to the number Betty had written on the message slip. In about a minute, a male voice boomed in my receiver.

"Mortar platoon. Sgt. Brown speaking. How may I help you, sir?"

"Yes, Sergeant, I need to speak to Corporal Charles hill. I'm calling long distance."

"Just a moment sir, I'll get him. I just saw him in the area."

I heard a rustle then a bump as the phone was laid down. I waited about five minutes before Chick Hill came on the line.

"Is this Matt Cole?" he asked. His voice sounded agitated.

"Yeah, it's me. what's wrong."

"I just wanted to tell you what a son of a bitch you are. Why did you tell Jenny that Ben Stole her bracelet?"

'Chick, she hired me to find the bracelet. I was just doing my job. Why? What happened."

"After you got done talking to her, Jenny called Ben in Las Vegas and really lit into him on the phone. She told him to come and get his shit out of her house and to never come back there. Ben got hot and they yelled at each other on the phone for a while until Jenny slammed down the phone on him and hung up. Ben took a charter plane to L.A. and came to the house two or three hours later and they resumed the argument. Finally, they got tired of yelling at each other and went to separate rooms like two boxers going to separate corners."

"The next morning the argument started up again. Jenny must have said something that pushed Ben over the line because he started pounding on her. As I told you before, Ben has hit Jenny a bunch of times. But this time was different. This time he hit her in the face. He blacked both of her eyes and loosened a couple of teeth. Jenny called me from the airport later on and said Ben Siegel had gone berserk on her and she was flying to Paris and never intended to see the son of a bitch again. All this happened because you told her about that fucking bracelet."

"I'm sorry Chick, but how was I to know this was going to happen?"

"The funny thing is, that Ben called me on the phone here at the base this morning. He told me he had sent Jenny on a trip to

Europe to look for classy paintings to hang on the walls of the Flamingo Hotel. He said he wouldn't be in Los Angeles this weekend, but invited me and my girlfriend out to dinner with him and one of his chums in L.A. on Friday the twentieth. Imagine the nerve of that bastard to invite me to dinner after working over my sister? I kept my cool though. I didn't let on that I knew what he had done," said Chick.

"I'm sorry this happened. If I knew about all this beforehand, I wouldn't have told your sister about the bracelet."

"Yeah, I know it wasn't your fault. I'm just mad at every son of a bitch in the world right now."

After finishing the call to Chick, I went in my closet and retrieved a pair of soft leather shoes with crepe soles I had forgotten I had. They would be much easier on my dogs as I continued my grid search. I left the office intending to go start my search again. While on the way, I changed my mind and drove to Virginia Hill's mansion instead.

I figured with Virginia in Europe and because it was mid-week, with Siegel in Las Vegas, the place might not be so well guarded and I might be able to get a peek inside the garage and find out what Vinnie Alfonsi was so anxious to hide. I parked my car in front of Virginia's mansion, took a small leather pouch from the glove compartment, and approached the front door. To my surprise, the door was opened not by the maid, but by Carlo the mountain and a half. When he saw who was at the door, he half-smiled at me and waved me inside.

"You all alone?" I asked.

"Just me and Solly here today. With the boss and Virginia gone I guess there isn't much to guard."

"Where's Solly," I asked.

"He snuck out to go see his girlfriend. Peeper, what the hell do you want?" asked the giant getting a little impatient.

"I want to get a look inside that locked garage out back."

"What for? They put new locks on all the doors and it's locked up tighter than Fort Knox. If you bust in there and do some damage doin it, it'll be my ass, when Vinnie comes back here and sees it."

"No worries," I said, holding up my little leather pouch. "Lockpicks. I can be in and out of there within five minutes and nobody but you and me will know."

"Will this help find Carmen?" he asked.

"Maybe so, maybe not. It's just a piece of the puzzle I'm trying to solve."

"Well, okay, go ahead."

I limped through the house, out the kitchen door, and across the rear lawn. I was confronted by three doors on the wall of the garage facing the house. Two of them was wide sliding doors to accommodate vehicles, secured with stout chains and even stouter padlocks. The third door was a regular pedestrian door secured by a shiny new Yale lock.

I knelt down with a groan and examined the lock. After checking the size of the key slot, I selected the appropriate pick from my collection and a tension bar. The pick was simply a tapered piece of sheet metal with a half-round bulge on the thin end. The tension bar was a narrow piece of spring steel bent in the shape of a letter "L."

Placing the tension bar in the key slot opposite the tumblers, I used my thumb to put tension on the lock cylinder. At the same time, I began to rake the tip of the lockpick repeatedly over the lock tumblers in the cylinder. After about thirty seconds of this, the lock suddenly sprang open and I turned the knob and entered the garage.

Even though it was broad daylight outside, it was semi-dark in the garage. After a few seconds, my eyes began to adjust to the darkness and I was able to find the light switch and turn on the overhead lights suspended from the ceiling.

It was just one huge space without walls or dividers of any kind. There was a lot of automobile-related junk hanging, or simply leaning on the inside walls. I walked around the space. There seemed to be a thick coating of dust on everything except one parking bay near the south end. This area looked like it had been recently swept and mopped. Why?

The Brat: "You should have brought a flashlight, you idiot."

I walked the entire cleaned up area looking at the floor. I found nothing. Then I noticed a large oil drip pan leaning against a toolbox just outside the cleaned area. The pan was stained and corroded with dirty oil and gunk. I took hold of its edge, careful not to get my hands too dirty, and flipped it around. I saw a fan-like spray of dark, rusty brown droplets that my experience told me was blood. Something really messy had happened to someone in that garage, and whoever had been assigned to clean up the mess had been lazy or incompetent. Not wanting to get their hands dirty with old grimy oil, instead of cleaning the blood off the drip pan, he (or it could have been a she, I suppose) simply turned it around to hide the blood spatter. I stood up and replaced the oil drip pan to its original position.

I turned off the light, backed out of the garage and relocked the door by turning the tension bar the opposite way I had turned it to open the lock. I went back into the house. On the way to the front door, I asked Carlo to write down the telephone number of the mansion. He wrote it on a piece of paper torn from the bottom of a menu from a local restaurant. I put it in my wallet as

I limped out to my car. But I didn't start my motor right away, but just sat and thought.

Captain Straight: "Someone was worked over pretty messily in that garage. The question is, did the victim survive the beating? Judging by the effort Siegel or someone in his employ went to hide the evidence, it suggests that the beatee didn't survive."

The Brat: "So Siegel rubbed out a guy. What's new about that. He probably misses his Murder Incorporated days and every now and then picks someone up at random, maybe a mailman or a Western Union boy, and beats him to death just for nostalgia."

Captain Straight: "Shut up. We don't need your wisecracks right now. Matt, maybe it's time we turned this whole case over to the police. It's obvious a murder has been committed."

The Brat: "Oh that's a brilliant suggestion. With a third of the cops taking bribes from Siegel, and another third taking money from Jack Dragna, there's a good chance you'll just be digging your own grave by reporting this."

I nodded my head, they were both right.

Captain straight: "As to who was murdered in that garage, my money is on Johnny Falcone, Jack Dragna's nephew who's missing and he is frantically searching for. That's why Siegel's men went to so much trouble to clean up the place after the murder. If Jack finds out that his favorite nephew was beaten to death in that garage, we'll have a gang war for sure."

The Brat: "Oh you think you're so smart. There could be another possible victim. It might be Carmen. We all thought that she ran away after seeing something that frightened her. But maybe she didn't run away at all. Maybe she was rubbed out by Siegel for screwing up his appointment calendar, wearing the wrong color nail polish or any number of other stupid reasons. The asshole just likes to pound on women."

I started my motor and drove out to 3rd and Highland and parked my Oldsmobile near the intersection.

§

As I turned the corner from the south side of 3rd to walk south on Mansfield, the fourth house down on the east side didn't look any different from its neighbors. No ray of sunlight popped out from behind a cloud and illuminated the house accompanied by organ music. There was no Maltese cross stenciled on the concrete walkway leading to the front door, and there wasn't a large sign in the front yard reading: "Wade's House," in big red letters with an arrow outlined in flashing lights pointing to the humble Craftsman-style abode. But it was Wade's house just the same.

I was limping my way along the sidewalk when an old Chevy with brown oxidized paint pulled up at the curb and parked a few houses ahead of me. A middle-aged guy wearing soiled khaki clothes and a union badge got out of the Chevy and walked wearily toward a house on the east side of the street, carrying a black lunch bucket. Hoping to save myself a few steps, I hailed him.

"Hey, mister, do you know of a family that lives around here named Perkins?" I asked as I was walking up to the man.

The guy stopped in his tracks and looked surprised. "Why, yes, my name is Charley Perkins, we just moved in here about four months ago," he replied.

"Do you have a twenty-year-old son name, Wade?"

The man's face seemed to fall apart and rearrange itself like a Chinese puzzle into an expression of dread and anxiety.

"Has something happened to Wade?" he asked like he was fearing the worst.

"Now hold on, I think Wade is okay right now, but if I'm right he could be in terrible danger."

We were interrupted by a woman coming out of the front door of the house. She was also middle-aged and frumpy with hair turning gray and a forehead wrinkled in concern. "Charley,"

she said, "who are you talking to? Does it have anything to do
with Wade?"

"Let me identify myself," I said and handed Charley Perkins
one of my business cards. "My name is Matthew Cole and I'm a
private investigator. I have some questions for your son Wade."

"I have some questions for him too, but I can't ask them.
Wade is missing and has been for weeks and I'm scared to death
he's mixed up with those gangsters he mows lawns for, that Siegel
guy," said Perkins.

"Can I come inside and discuss this with you?"

"Yeah, sure, follow me." the three of us then went inside and
Charley Perkins and I sat at a chrome and vinyl kitchen table
while Mrs. Perkins fussed around us making coffee.

"When is the last time either of you saw your son," I asked.

"On May seventeenth. I wasn't here but Martha, my wife was.
She told me Wade came bustling in here and went straight to his
room. He came out a few minutes later carrying his rucksack. It
was stuffed full of clothes and stuff, I guess. He told his mother
that he had to go on a trip and for her not to worry if we didn't
hear from him. Martha keeps some cash hidden in a can here in
the kitchen. Wade took that, kissed his mom on the cheek and
hurried out. I didn't realize until a couple of days later that he

also took my father's old gun from a drawer in our bedroom. It's a .22 Colt, Woodsman with a four-inch barrel."

Mrs. Perkins brought two steaming cups of coffee to the table along with a creamer and a sugar bowl, with a silver spoon.

"It's all your fault for letting him work for those gangsters," said Mrs. Perkins to her husband.

"Hells bells, woman, he isn't ten years old anymore. He's a grown man. I couldn't tell him what to do even if I wanted to," he replied.

"In the days before he left, did Wade talk about meeting or seeing a new girl?" I asked. Charley and Martha Perkins both shook their heads. But Charley had a question for me.

"Who are you working for mister?

"I'm working for the brother of a girl named Carmen, and I think she might be with Wade.

Do either of you have any idea where Wade would go if he wanted to hide out and not be found?"

They thought for a while then shook their heads again.
"Does Wade have a car?"

"Yeah, he owns a 1934 Ford pickup truck painted blue. He did the paint job himself with a borrowed spray gun," said Mr. Perkins.

"Do you know the plate number?" I asked.

"I got it here someplace, " he said and rummaged around in a kitchen drawer. "Yeah, it's 38M227." I wrote the number down in my notebook.

"Well, you have my card. if you should think of anything else or come up with a place where he might be hiding, call the number on the card. If I'm not there, leave a detailed message with the girl who answers the phone, okay?"

They nodded their heads in unison. As I was walking out the door, Mrs. Perkins stopped me. "Mister, I don't know who you really are or how you figure in all this, but please find my boy and bring him back to me," she said with tears in the corners of her eyes.

As I limped back to where my car was parked I was feeling discouraged. Nothing was going right with the case. I felt like I was just spinning my wheels and going nowhere. The only bright spot in my outlook was the fact that I wouldn't have to go house to house anymore. If my feet could have talked, they would have thanked me.

CHAPTER TWELVE

LOS ANGELES
JUNE 1I, 1947
WEDNESDAY
1:30 P.M.

I was standing on Highland Avenue, just south of 3rd Street near the driver's door of my car fishing in my pocket for my keys. Just then a long black Buick sedan roared up and stopped abruptly in the street beside me. I could see two men in the front and several more in the rear passenger compartment. The rear door of the Buick swung open and I saw a nattily dressed little man with a face that looked like a rat, perched on the fold-down jump seat just inside the rear compartment of the Buick.

"Get in," he ordered.

Now I don't usually don't just hop in cars with strange men dressed like gangsters. In fact, it's listed as "don't" # five in the Official Private Eye Handbook of Dos and Don'ts. But in this case, "don't" # five was overruled by "don't" # three, which stated:

"don't refuse any requests from a guy who has a thirty-eight revolver pointed at your belly-button."

As I climbed in the back seat of the Buick, the rat-faced guy holding the revolver on me backed up further into the interior and I replaced him on the jump seat. There were two rough-looking men seated on the rear seat in addition to rat face. That meant, without my having to look down and count on my fingers, that I was in a car with five L.A. mobsters. As to what faction, Siegel or Dragna, my new friends were from was an open question. Because they didn't wear mob identity badges, telling who was who, it was kind of hard to tell at first glance, kind of like telling the difference between Quaker quick oats and regular Quaker Oats.

Ratface reached out, grabbed my lapel and jerked me down on the floor of the rear seat. He frisked me where I lay, using one hand while still holding the gun with the other. He removed my gun and wallet and put both in the breast pocket of his two hundred dollar suit.

"Keep yer head down and don't look around. If you don't do as I want, I'll plug you," he said.

Since "do" # 17 of the handbook said: "Do what a guy wants you to do if he says to you: 'If you don't do as I want, I'll plug you,'" I did what he wanted.

The Brat: "You're getting a little too cute there, even for me, stop it."

I saw a movie once where Robert Young was in my exact same predicament, though with him it was Nazi spies and not gangsters. What he did was memorize the turns of the car he was in and noted any bumps and railroad tracks along the way so he could later lead the FBI to the spies. I didn't do that. Why you might ask. Because that was a movie and this was real life, not some Hollywood bullshit.

The trip lasted for about half an hour. The gangsters in the car were silent as we drove, except for the usual farts and belches you get from guys eating Italian food all the time. When the car stopped and I was jerked upright, I saw that we were parked in an alley in a business district. I could see garbage cans and paper trash strewn along the bottoms of the boards of wooden fences. I was jerked roughly out of the car and through a metal door. The six of us strode down a dingy hallway to an open door on the left. Ratface went inside.

"We brought him, boss, just like you said," I heard him say.

"Bring the gentleman in," said another voice, much more cultured than rat face,s ugly snarl. I was brought into the room by two goons, each holding an arm and shoved into a chair. I found myself facing a man across a scarred desk. I saw my Colt pistol and my wallet laying on the desk in front of him. as I watched, he picked up my gun, pushed the magazine release and the magazine dropped into the hand not holding the gun. Next, he pulled back the slide ejecting the cartridge from the chamber and locked back the slide. He then gently laid the pistol back down.

If I had seen him on the street, I would have guessed that this guy was a stockbroker or high-end businessman. He was about forty wearing a meticulously tailored business suit with waistcoat, not nearly as flashy as ratface's. His hair was neatly trimmed and he wore horn-rim glasses. I saw a big diamond in a gold ring on his right pinky finger.

"Under ordinary circumstances," the man began, "when two gentlemen meet, they first introduce themselves. But I think in this case that we can dispense with that formality. I already know who you are and you have no need to know who I am. All you need to know is I'm a lawyer representing the interests of a prominent businessman here in Los Angeles. His name is Jack Dragna."

"On three occasions, you were seen entering and leaving Virginia Hill's house in Beverly Hills. What was your purpose for being there?"

I paused before speaking. I was considering how much to tell this man.

"Captain Straight: "Tell him all of it. You don't owe any loyalty to Bugsy Siegel."

"As you know I'm a private Investigator. Virginia Hill hired me to find a stolen diamond bracelet. On my first visit, I interviewed Miss Hill and the servants. On the second visit I told her who had stolen the bracelet and also told her why I couldn't recover it for her," I said.

"Who stole the bracelet?" asked the lawyer.

"Mr. Ben Siegel himself. He took it to give to one of his other girlfriends."

"Interesting," said the lawyer after a little chuckle. But then his face turned serious. "So that was the only reason you went to the house?"

"No," I replied, "Without Virginia Hill's or Ben Siegel's knowledge, I was also trying to find a missing girl. Her name is Carmen Cardello. Siegel brought her to California from Las Vegas and soon after she disappeared. Her Brother Tony hired me to find her."

"Tony Cardello? Siegel's pit boss in Las Vegas? Have you found her?"

" Yes, yes, and not yet."

The lawyer nodded and then pushed a five by seven-inch photograph over the desk to me. I picked it up. It showed a young face, maybe early twenties with curly hair giving a wise-ass, cocky look for the camera.

"The man in that photograph is named Johnny Falcone. During your time in Virginia Hill's home, did you ever see him, or hear his name discussed."

"No," I lied. I didn't want to repeat what Solly had said about Falcone.

"You're not being very helpful Mr. Cole. Mr. Dragna is very anxious to find his nephew. It would be in your interest to give us something, anything that might solve the riddle of Johnny Falcone's disappearance. It might mean the difference between my associates out in the hall taking you back to your automobile, dusting you off, and letting you go, or taking you to a much more unpleasant place. Understood?"

I figured this was all bullshit. The lawyer was just trying to intimidate me. Jack Dragna must be shitting bricks desperate to find Falcone for this cultured asshole to haul me in here and lean on me hard like this. Well. I was about to give him something that would definitely raise his blood pressure and might possibly start a gang war.

"When I was at Virginia's house the first time, I asked if I could examine the room that Carmen Cardello had occupied before her disappearance. After looking at the room, I came downstairs and noticed that the garage itself had new locks on the doors and was sealed tight. One of Siegel's bodyguards, Vinnie Alfonsi, caught me looking in the garage window, got angry and shooed me away."

"The reason I went back to Virginia's house the third time was to pick one of the locks to find out why Vinnie was so protective of the inside of that garage. I found blood spatter in there. Somebody was worked over pretty messily in that garage. I'm not sure who the victim was. It could have been Carmen Cardello or someone totally unrelated who pissed off Ben Siegel. But it also might have been Johnny Falcone."

He tried to conceal it but I saw the excitement dance in the lawyer's eyes. "Okay, You're off the hook. I'll have the boys drive you back to your car."

CHAPTER THIRTEEN

LOS ANGELES
JUNE 13, 1947
FRIDAY
10:00 A.M.

A s the clock on my desk showed ten A.M. on the dot, I
sipped my Hillbilly coffee, took a long drag on a Camel
cigarette and exhaled the smoke. I called my morning
alcoholic concoction Hillbilly coffee because it was a mixture of
Jack Daniel's bourbon and burnt office coffee and was a
backwoods imitation of the posher Irish coffee that the swells
drank. While sitting at my desk in my private office, I was poring
over the morning edition of the Los Angeles Times. I was
looking for any mention or gossip about the Dragna gang's
reaction to the news I gave them on Wednesday. There had been
nothing in the paper the previous day. In fact, nothing had
happened on Thursday. Even Mrs. Adderley had left me alone.
The hiatus didn't bother me, sometimes cases were like that. You
make significant progress for several days running and then
wham, everything comes to a screeching halt. I didn't fight it, I
just used the off day to rest up from my labors of the previous

week. Anyway, to tell the truth, I had hit a stone wall as far as finding Carmen was concerned.

Mrs. Adderley came breezing into my office with a bustling, professional air. Luann followed her in as usual. But Luann appeared different. She seemed almost calm with a dreamy smile on her face.

The Brat: "Do you think Luann got ahold of some happy pills someplace? In her condition, if she tries to take off and go into her usual hover, she might fly out of a window, fall three stories and hurt herself."

"Mr. Cole, Here is the balance sheet of the company for June," said Mrs. Adderley as she handed me a sheet of paper while wearing a smug little smile. "As you can see, we did very well last month, very well indeed."

The Brat: "That makes two days now that that lady has walked around grinning at you like a Cheshire cat. She's up to something. Are you sure you checked all the drawers for rattlesnakes?"

The Brat was right, I could feel it. The lady did have something up her sleeve.

"Mrs. Adderley, you haven't been having little chats with people behind my back, have you? Like maybe with the IRS?" I asked.

The Brat; "Aha! You better run out and buy a jar of Vaseline right now. Those IRS goons could be on the way over here right now."

"Mr. Cole, I can't figure out if you are full-blown crazy or just a trifle paranoid. I just so happens that I have decided that I was maybe too pushy with you in the past and I intend to ease up on you from now on," said my office manager.

The brat: "Don't believe her, she's just trying to lull you into a false sense of security to keep you from running for the border before the feds show up."

"That was unkind of me, Mrs. Adderley and I apologize. That was great news about the balance sheet. I'm sure it's all due to your good management. But then again, Mussolini was able to get the Italian trains to run on time, at least at first," I said.

"Good lord," said Mrs. Adderley, rolling her eyes, before turning on her heel and stalking out with Luann stumbling after her.

I finished going through the newspaper. There was nothing in there about a police investigation of the disappearance of Johnny Falcone. My intercom buzzed. I hit the right button the first time.

"Mr. Cole, there's a man here to see you. He says he is Sergeant Whitmore of the Beverly Hills Police Department."

"Send him in Betty. Things were getting kind of dull around here anyway," I replied.

The man who walked into my office didn't have to announce himself as a cop. It was written all over him. From his cheap, sagging suit, to his scuffed rubber-soled shoes and the disgusted, frustrated expression on his face. He was on the cloudy side of forty with a lined, craggy face and eyes that made me feel he could see that pimple on my hip I discovered that morning, right through my clothes. I liked him at first glance.

"Good morning, Sgt. Whitmore, come in and have a seat. I was about to have a drink to kill the germs from this unhealthy office air. Care to join me," I asked.

"Don't mind if I do. It is kind of stuffy in here isn't it," the sergeant replied as he sat down across from me. I retrieved my whiskey bottle and two glasses, one dirty, one clean. I gave the clean one with two fingers of amber liquid in it to the cop. we held up our glasses in a silent toast to each other and drank.

"Cole, I got a tip that there might have been a killing in the garage of Virginia Hill's mansion in my town. The tip came from a lawyer I know who I also know is connected pretty tight to Jack Dragna and the Chicago boys. He, the lawyer, snitched you off and said that the information came from you. I don't know if you're aware of it yet but you're getting into some pretty deep waters here."

"Understood," I replied.

I got a search warrant from a very compliant judge I know on the q.t. and raided the place with some of my men yesterday afternoon about dusk. There were only two of Siegel's goons on the grounds of the mansion. One was a guy about seven feet tall and the wider than a grain elevator. The other was normal sized but looked like Tiny Tim standing next to the first guy. They didn't interfere once I showed them the search warrant."

At this point, the sergeant paused and leaned forward in his chair.

"We found all kinds of evidence that somebody was beaten within an inch of his life or maybe killed in that garage. About the only thing the lab could tell us about the blood we found was that it was "O" positive. Which gets me nowhere, half the people in the Los Angeles area have O positive blood. The lawyer who gave me the original tip about this thinks the blood belongs to Johnny Falcone. So far I've been able to keep any mention of this out of the newspaper. What I need to know from you is how you came to know about all this."

So I told Sergeant Whitmore everything. I talked and talked so much that at the end I was so parched from talking that I had to pour myself another wee dram of bourbon and drink it down. All the while I was talking, the cop just stared at me with weary eyes and didn't interrupt.

"How close are you to finding this Carmen girl's whereabouts?" Whitmore asked.

"Right now I'm at a dead end. I don't have a clue about where she is."

"Well, you might not ever find her. I learned about a new wrinkle this morning. Two guys named Louie Gaetti and Tony Fieri, two small-time grifters with a rap sheet long enough to wrap completely around the equator, have told certain members of the Chicago mob that they saw Johnny Falcone alive and well, drinking in a bar on the south side of Chicago with a blonde dame yesterday evening. If what they say is true, and that's a big if, then I'd lay bets that the victim of this crime is probably the girl you're searching for, Carmen Cardello."

After Sgt. Whitmore left my office I sat and thought about my next move. I was perplexed because I didn't think there was the next move for me to locate Carmen. My intercom suddenly buzzed and I hit the button.

"Mr. Cole. You have a call on line two. The caller says it's urgent."

I picked up the receiver of my desk phone and punched the blinking button for line two.

"Matt Cole," I said.

"Do you recognize my voice," said the caller. I did. It was Tony Cardello.

"Yes."

"You need to get the hell out of there and go to ground right now. I overheard the boss talking on the phone. He found out from a spy that you told the opposition about the garage. The boss has ordered a hit on you. Guys are on their way over there right now," Tony said and clicked off.

I didn't hesitate. Inside of thirty seconds, I was downstairs and unlocking my car. Ten seconds after that, I was driving east on Wilshire. My first stop was at my bank where I withdrew a thousand dollars in tens and twenties. I couldn't fit all the cash in my wallet, so I had to put some of it in the side pockets of my suit jacket. Next, I drove to a large service garage on Olympic and Crenshaw and turned into their lot. A service attendant greeted me while wiping his hands on a greasy rag.

'How can I help you, mister?"

"I need to store my car for a week or so. Can you do that?" I asked.

"Sure, I guess so. We don't store cars that often but I think we can handle it. We'll have to charge you a dollar a day though."

"That will be fine.," I said and paid ten dollars in advance as an attendant drove my car around to the back of the building. I walked back out to the street and hailed a passing cab. I told the driver to take me to the nearest used car lot. He took me to a place called "Manny's Motors" on Pico. It was a big lot with about a hundred used cars parked on it. I paid the cab driver and approached a wooden shack labeled, "Office," that sat among the used cars like an island in a sea of multicolored metal. Before I could get within twenty feet of the shack, a car salesman bolted from its door and greeted me like I was his long lost uncle just miraculously returned from an expedition up the Amazon River. The salesman was middle-aged and skinny, wearing a pinstriped suit that was a size too big for him, a white shirt with a collar too large for his pencil neck, slicked-back hair, and a thin mustache.

"Lookin' for a car? Well, mister, you sure come to the right place. Look around you and take your pick. They're all in A-1 top condition and we're giving them away at half the prices other lots charge. Why take this beauty here," he said and pointed at a late model Ford sedan near where we were standing. "This fine Ford has only had one owner, has low miles and drives like a dream. It was owned by an elderly lady who only took it out of the garage on Sundays to drive a few miles to see her sister."

The Brat: " Yeah, her sister was probably an inmate at the Tehachapi Woman's prison and they spend the whole afternoon chatting about her sister's wonderful new job in the laundry."

The guy finally stopped talking to take a breath. Before he could start up again, I said, " I'm looking for something dependable but I don't have a lot of money."

The salesman's face fell for just a second and was then was again instantly replaced by his phony smile. 'Well, my friend," he said, "why don't we take a stroll around the lot and find a car that strikes your fancy."

I followed the salesman as we zig-zagged from one end of the lot to the other, while he babbled non-stop. Finally, in the back row of cars, I spotted what I wanted.

The car was a 1936 Hudson, four-door sedan. Its once glossy white paint was oxidized to the point that it resembled the yellowish color and texture of a towel in a Skid row Turkish bath. I looked at the inside of the car through a side window. The interior of the heap was stained and threadbare, but I didn't see any springs poking through the cloth of the seats. Surprisingly, the tires were pretty good, with plenty of tread. I asked the salesman if I could start up the motor. He retrieved the keys to the Hudson, which had been hidden above the sun visor, and handed them to me. Seating myself behind the wheel, I saw that the car had seventy-six thousand miles on it. I turned on the key and hit the starter button on the dash.

The car sprang to life with a healthy roar. Hudson's had a reputation of being well built and reliable. The only problem they were said to have was a propensity to wear out piston rings faster than the taps on Shirley Temple's shoes. Excessively worn piston rings caused the engine to blow out blue smoke from the exhaust pipe. It wasn't unusual to see a Hudson tooling down the street belching out more smoke than a Fletcher-class destroyer laying down a smokescreen. To check for this, I revved the motor a couple of times and then looked back behind the car. No blue smoke. I shut off the motor and got out.

'How Much?" I asked.

"I can let you have this fine, dependable car for one hundred twenty-nine dollars and ninety-nine cents, plus tax of course."

"A hundred and thirty bucks for a 36 Hudson with almost eighty thousand miles on it? C'mon, I'll give you eighty-five," I offered.

From the car salesman's expression, you'd have thought that I had just broken into his house, raped his wife, and jerked out his little girl's tongue root and all. "I can go maybe, one-ten," he replied.

I limped over to the front of the Hudson near the headlight and sighted down the length of its side. "Come over here and look at this," I said. "Look at that sheet metal. It has more waves in it than the Sea of Cortez and the inside of this heap looks like it was lived in by an old crazy woman with ninety inbred pet cats. I'll tell you what. I'll give you a hundred bucks flat, no tax. My final offer," I said.

Captain Straight: "What's the matter with you, Matt? You have gangsters roaming the streets looking for you to fill you full of holes, and here you are haggling with a car salesman over twenty-five bucks."

The Brat: " You're getting as fussy and impatient lately as an old maid who misplaced her vibrator. Doing fun shit like this is the reason for living."

"Okay, but at that price, you'll have to take it to the DMV and register it yourself. Will that be cash or check?"

"Cash."

"Okay, I'll go get the pink slip," replied the salesman.

I discovered that the car drove surprisingly well when I gunned the motor and took off west on Pico Boulevard. Apart from a little shimmy at thirty-five mph, the Hudson handled just fine. I drove around for a while, looking for a particular kind of store.

The Brat: " About time for a little drink isn't it? I'm parched from all that haggling with the car salesman."

Captain straight: "Why are you parched. Matt did all the haggling while you just cracked jokes. Anyway, we left the office in such a hurry Matt forgot to grab the whiskey bottle. We're lucky he remembered his gun."

The Brat: "He should have grabbed the bottle and forgot the gun. If those gangsters catch up with us, one gun isn't going to matter. Whereas, if we had the bottle, at least we would be feeling very relaxed and mellow as they're filling us full of holes."

The bastard kept needling me on and on about getting a drink. Finally, I stopped at a liquor store and bought a fifth of Jack Daniel's and two cartons of Camels. After I took a healthy swig, The Brat quieted down. I turned north on Figueroa and saw a Sears & Roebuck store ahead on the right.

I parked in the parking lot in front of the store. I went in and bought four sets of khaki work pants and shirts. I also bought a pair of clodhopper work boots, a dozen pairs of jockey shorts, heavy cotton socks, and a blue baseball cap. With my khaki work clothes, my baseball cap and beat up heap, I hoped I looked like just another working Joe, like thousands of others in Los Angeles. Another stop was at an Owl Drug Store where I bought shaving gear, soap and other toiletries encased in a cheap leatherette case. I changed clothes in a gas station washroom and put my wadded up suit in the trunk of the Hudson. Keeping north on Figueroa, I drove until I came to Route 66 in Pasadena, then turned right and pointed the rocket-shaped hood ornament of my Hudson east.

CHAPTER FOURTEEN

AZUSA
JUNE 13, 1947
FRIDAY
7:50 P.M.

The sun was just about to set as I drove into the little town of Azusa. The town was about twenty-five miles from the Los Angeles city hall and was about the last place that I thought Bugsy Siegel's goons would think to look for me. Route 66 through Azusa was lined with motor courts and small cafés and restaurants, interspersed every now and then with a gas station or a gift shop. About a hundred yards past the "Welcome To Azusa" sign, I saw a motor hotel that looked like it was newer than the others around it. The neon sign projecting from its roof declared it to be the "Rest-eezy Motor hotel." I pulled into the lot in front of the sign. The place consisted of an office and a line of individual cottages with a parking place beside each stretching out behind. I got out of the Hudson and went inside the office.

There were two people inside. One was a pudgy guy in his early thirties wearing a checked shirt. The only things that stood out about him were his crew-cut hair, with spikes standing straight up in the front and the big smile on his round face. The other person in the office was a slim woman in a maid's uniform with dark shoulder-length hair, standing and looking out a window with her back turned to me. She was smoking a cigarette and flicking the ashes toward a big glass ashtray perched on a table nearby. When I entered the office the woman turned around and glanced at me before turning away again. My brief look at her revealed a narrow, pinched face with hostile eyes.

"Hi, mister, My name is Bill Watson. Need a room? Well, you come to the right place. Our rooms are clean as a whistle with the best beds on Route 66. Martha here is my wife." He said, motioning toward the woman behind him. "When we bought this place we swore we were going to provide travelers the best overnight experience they ever had."

The woman muttered a sentence under her breath. I had always had extremely good hearing. She thought I wasn't able to hear what she was saying, but I caught every word.

"Bullshit, we got most of our beds from a fire sale at an old folk's home."

"Are you interested in just one night or will you be staying longer?" asked smiling Bill.

"Hah, that's a laugh. One night in this dump and he'll be gone before dawn," muttered the woman.

"I may be here a few days, I'm not sure," I replied.

Smiling Bill turned to a rack of keys. "Well, I'll put you in cabin number seven. It's one of our best rooms. The rate is three dollars a night and that's a bargain believe you me. Just give us a half-hour or so for Martha to put the finishing touches on your room. While you wait, if you're hungry you might try the 'Over-Easy Café' across the street. They serve great chicken fried steak."

"Finishing touches my ass. I'll have to make the bed, clean up the bathroom and chase out the cockroaches. All I do is drudge work. But hell, that's what I get for marrying a loser," muttered Martha.

The Brat: "How'd you like to be married to that. Can you imagine having sex with that for fifty-years? Now I know why guys join the French Foreign Legion."

Little Matt: " Huh, did I hear somebody mention 'having sex?'"

The Brat: "Go back to sleep stupid."

Little Matt: " I distinctly heard someone say something about having sex."

The Brat; "The word you heard was 'sax.' We were talking about buying a saxophone, a harmonica, and a tuba and starting a one-man band."

Little Matt: "Oh, okay."

On my way across the street to check out the Over-easy Café, I stopped at the edge of the street and surveyed the building around me.

The Brat: "You know Azusa isn't bad. We got a place to sleep and a place to eat. If one of these other building turns out to be a whorehouse, we might never have to leave at all."

I spent the rest of the evening listening to the radio in my cabin and working my way through my fifth of bourbon and cartons of Camel cigarettes. The Over-easy Café had turned out to be adequate. The so-so quality of the food was offset by the enormous portions served. The room also turned out to be okay, despite Martha's mutterings.

§

I was awakened by the peculiar aroma of Guadalcanal Island. The smell was a mix of rotten vegetation, Cordite and the peculiar sickly sweet reek of rotting human flesh. I looked around me and saw that I was in a fighting hole with a Browning Automatic rifle in my hands and my dead friend "Pickle" beside me in the hole. The mud of the cleared jungle in front of me was littered with the corpses of hundreds of Japanese soldiers who had died trying to breach the thin Marine line. But the battlefield was silent and I wondered why. I looked down the line of Marine holes to my right and left. All the men in them appeared to be as dead as the Japanese to my front.

Was it possible that I was the last human left alive on this battlefield south of Henderson Field?

I started to climb out of the hole. I had to see about this. Someone must be alive who can tell me what the situation is. Maybe the officers behind the line would know something.

I detected movement at the edge of the jungle about sixty yards in front of me. I ducked back down in the hole and grabbed my BAR again. I concentrated on the spot where I had seen the movement and saw a single Japanese Soldier emerge from the jungle and begin picking his way among the corpses of his comrades. The soldier was wearing a khaki uniform and a mushroom helmet and was carrying a rifle with a long fixed bayonet. He was coming straight toward me. I raised my BAR, sighted on the soldier and pulled the trigger. But there was no boom of the big.30 caliber round going off, no kickback of the heavy weapon against my shoulder. There was only a loud metallic bang as the bolt slammed forward on an empty chamber.

I jerked the magazine from the BAR and saw that it was empty. I frantically searched around in the hole for a loaded one. But it was no use. There was no ammunition anywhere I searched. Even the small clips for my pistol were empty. As I saw that the soldier was getting much closer, a feeling of foreboding came over me. I realized I had no weapon to defend myself from the Japanese. I scrambled out of the hole, thinking to charge the Japanese, and maybe pick up some sort of weapon on the way. But when I tried to take my first step forward, my left leg collapsed under me.

Then a weird thing began to happen. When he was about twenty feet from me, the Japanese soldier started to transform before my eyes. Instead of a khaki uniform and rifle, he was wearing a pinstriped, blue suit and he was carrying a Tommy gun with a big drum magazine and a vertical forward grip. The soldier's face was changing too. Instead of an Asian face, I now saw the handsome, smiling face of Bugsy Siegel.

"Did you really think you could rat me out and get away with it?" asked Siegel.

"No. Wait," I said, as he raised the Tommy gun into firing position. I saw the barrel if the weapon erupt with flashes and sound. I knew that I had less than a split-second to live.

I sat up in bed gasping for air and drenched in sweat. My eyes darted around the room and I panicked upon seeing the unfamiliar surroundings.

Captain Straight: "It's only a nightmare. You're okay. Pull yourself together."

It took two Camel cigarettes and a couple of healthy pulls on the neck of my whiskey bottle to get my blood pressure out of the danger zone.

The Brat; "I guess we'll have to suspend the 'no drinking whiskey except out of a glass" rule for the duration of this case."

I rubbed my face with both hands. I had been cooped up in that small room for five days and I was going batty. I decided I had to get out for a little while. I Shaved and dressed in my day laborer costume and limped across the street to Over-Easy Café for breakfast. I was served enough pancakes to fill up Paul Bunyan, his sawmill crew, Babe the Blue Ox, Babe's wife Babette and all the little baby blue oxen.

After breakfast, I went back across the street and paid my bill for the previous night. I had been paying daily, not knowing if I would have to leave suddenly and not come back. For the same reason, I put my shaving kit and change of clothes in the trunk of my Hudson every day.

I drove back west on Route 66 until I got to Pasadena. I drove around until I spotted a phonebooth that was in the shade of a gnarled old oak tree. I retrieved my roll of nickels from the pocket of my rolled-up suit in the trunk of the Hudson, limped to the phonebooth and dialed my office.

"A-1 Discrete Detective Agency. This is Betty, how may I help you?"

"Betty, this is Matt Cole."

"Oh, Mr. Cole, we've been so worried about you. Just a moment, Mrs. Adderley gave orders that she was to be notified if you called in. Just a moment."

Betty clicked off and there were about fifteen seconds of dead air. Then Mrs. Adderley came on the line.

"Mr. Cole, Where have you been? I've suspended operations in the office and have had all our detectives out looking for you."

"Looking for me Mrs. Adderley, whatever for?"

"On Friday, a few minutes after you rushed out of here, three shady-looking men barged in here demanding to know where you were. I told them that your whereabouts were none of their concern. They tried to intimidate me but were persuaded to leave when four of our detectives came out of their cubicles and stood behind me."

I had a silent laugh at Siegel's hit squad going up against Mrs. Adderley. Didn't those fools know they were outclassed?

"Those guys who barged in there were probably Russian NKVD goons. I broke into the locked cabinet where Stalin keeps his personal Vodka. I discovered that it was distilled by Russian immigrants in St. Louis, Missouri. Stalin's goons are desperate to silence me. If the Russian people were to ever find out that their dear, "Uncle Koba," is drinking American Vodka, there'll be a second Russian revolution. They might even appoint a new Tsar and beg to be serfs again." I said.

"Mr. Cole, this is no time for stupid jokes. Should I call the police?"

"No, no police. Don't worry, I'll figure out what I'm working on sooner or later and we can resume our normal operations. As for right now, put Betty back on the phone."

"Yes, Mr. Cole?" asked Betty tentatively.

"Has anyone called and left a message for me. Maybe a Sgt. Whitmore?"

"No, sir, no Sgt. Whitmore. But a Mr. Perkins called this morning. He said he's remembered something. He doesn't have a phone but he said if you come by his house after four, he'll talk to you. Mr. Perkins left his address, it's …"

I stopped her. "I know where he lives Betty. I'll call you tomorrow and check for more messages."

CHAPTER FIFTEEN

LOS ANGELES
JUNE 18, 1947
WEDNESDAY
1:30 P.M.

When Charley Perkins saw me through the screen door he frowned. "Why are you dressed like that?" He asked as he let me in.

"I'm working undercover on a case. What did you call me about?"

"Come on into the kitchen. It will take some explaining," said Perkins.

I sat down at the table in the same seat I had occupied the last time I interviewed Charley. Mrs. Perkins brought me a cup of coffee just like last time. Mr. Perkins took a sip and then started talking.

"In 1919, a big timber company cut down all the trees, left nothin' but stumps, on a big chunk of land they owned just north of the new Lake Arrowhead development. Once the trees were cut, the land was useless to the company until the trees grew back. Then I guess somebody in the company got a idea. The company subdivided that land into five-acre parcels and offered them to the public as recreational leases. The leases were to last until the trees on the land averaged over sixty feet tall or forty years, whichever occurred first. The suckers who bit on this scheme were allowed to cut a road to a homesite and build a one-story cabin, but they not allowed to change the contours of the land or cut any new trees springing up. They sold some leases and it looked like the whole stupid idea would pan out nicely. Then there was an economic panic in 1920. Sales of the lots in the Lake Arrowhead development dried up and so did the leases for the timber company land."

"In Fact, sales of the leases got so bad that my dad, who had inherited a little money from my grandpa, leased one of the five-acre parcels from the timber company for twenty-five dollars in December 1920. You see, my dad had this idea that he would turn those five acres of stumps into a beautiful retreat for the Perkins family. Every weekend he would drag us kids up there to work on his road, or help clear and level the homesite. By the middle of 1921, we had succeeded in building a structure on our five acres of stumps. My dad called it his cabin. But it was really just a shack, with no electricity or running water. My mom, as well as us kids, hated it, so we didn't go there much when we got older.'

"The reason I'm telling you all this is that when Wade was a youngster, maybe nine or ten, he spent a lot of time up at that shack with my father. The two of them would go up there on weekends and longer stretches during the summer. They would rough it and sleep in the shack. Anyway, I don't think anybody has been up there since my dad died about five years ago. Maybe I'm wasting your time and I know it's a long shot. I guess that's why I didn't think of it till the other day. I have to work all week or I'd go up there myself and save you the trouble," said Charley Perkins and bowed his head.

"How do you get to this shack?" I asked

"From the Lake Arrowhead lodge, drive around the lake to the north shore. Keep angling north till you find Yosemite Drive. Drive north till it dead ends. Angling off to the right will be an unmarked dirt road. Follow it but be careful, it's kinda rough. About eighty yards down that road, you'll see the shack on your right."

After I thanked Charley Perkins, I got back in my Hudson and fled east on Route 66 again, heading back to my hotel room in Azusa. It was too late in the day to start up to Charley's cabin. I had no wish to drive narrow, treacherous mountain roads in the dark. Once again I dined at the Over-Easy Café. I had pot roast this time. The flavor was not bad but the meat was as tough as a Marine drill instructor cooked medium-rare.

The next morning I was up early. I opted for a detectives breakfast instead of the massive meals served at the Over-Easy Café. A traditional police detective's breakfast consisted of two cups of black coffee, four cigarettes, and two aspirin tablets. But I modified mine somewhat. I put cream in my coffee. After putting my meager belongings in the trunk of my car, and paying my room rent for the final time, I fired up the Hudson and pointed the rocket on the hood east on Route 66.

Because it was a weekday morning most of the traffic on the highway was going the other way, toward Los Angeles. I made pretty good time in long, empty stretches of semi-desert. But each little town I drove through, Glendora, Claremont, Cucamonga, had stop signs at every one of the streets Route 66 crossed. I understood why the town fathers put up those stop signs. It was an effort to slow travelers down and maybe get them to patronize the businesses lining the road.

In Cucamonga, I noticed that I needed gas. I pulled into a Standard station and told the attendant to fill up my tank. While he and his helper filled my tank, cleaned my windshield, checked my engine oil level and measured the air pressure in my tires, I went to the washroom and relieved myself. Afterward, I wandered into the office where I saw collections of free maps. I took one off a stack labeled "Southern California" and unfolded it. I traced the route to Lake Arrowhead with my index finger, then refolded the map and put it in my pocket.

As I entered San Bernardino, Route 66 also became Foothill Boulevard. According to the map, I was to stay on Foothill after Route 66 swings north toward Barstow and look for a sign for Highway 18 north.

The Brat: " I got this weird feeling that we're being followed."

Captain Straight: "What have you seen that gives you that impression?"

The Brat: "I haven't seen shit. I just got this feeling."

For the next couple of miles, I kept my eye on the rearview mirror keeping track of the cars and trucks behind me. I finally concluded that if I was being tailed, it was by an expert. Just to make sure, at the next cross street, I gunned my motor and did a sliding right turn. After recovering from the turn, I hit the gas again and barreled at high speed for two blocks and turned left. I continued to make random turns at high speed through a residential area of San Bernardino. I hoped some housewife didn't pick that particular time to take her baby for a walk on a quiet street. After eight or nine turns, I stomped on the brakes, pulled to the curb, slid down in my seat and waited.

A big black car didn't rush by containing ten gangster goons with their heads swiveling in all directions looking for my Hudson. Joseph Stalin didn't get up in front of the Communist Party Congress and announce: "I'm sorry comrades, we've tried it, but Communism just doesn't work. We must return to

Capitalism as soon as possible so I can finally get my toilet fixed."
Katherine Hepburn didn't call a press conference and admit that
the reason she has so many male mannerisms is that she's really
Bert Lahr dressed in drag. The Democrats and Republicans in
Washington didn't get together and issue a joint statement saying
they were going to put politics aside and finally do something for
the good the American people. In short, nothing happened. I
returned to Route 66 and continued my journey.

Captain Straight: "Are you satisfied now? You've wasted our
time."

The Brat: "What can I say? I still have this feeling."

I saw the sign for Highway 18 in time to poke my arm out my
window and signal a left turn for the drivers behind me. Highway
18 took me into the foothills of the San Bernardino Mountains
and was blacktop for about ten miles before it abruptly turned to
gravel. The ascent into the mountains was hair raising. The
narrow gravel road clung to the sides of the mountains and made
numerous switchback turns. Concentration was imperative
because there were no guard rails to protect against drops of
thousands of feet. There wasn't much traffic. I looked behind me
and saw only a white Ford about eighty yards to my rear. Upon
reaching a plateau at the top of the mountain, the road became
less steep and headed north again. I breathed a sigh of relief.

After about an hour and a half on the mountain road, I began
to get drowsy and almost missed the sign announcing the turnoff

for Lake Arrowhead. When I made the turn, I looked back and saw that the white Ford didn't follow me, but continued on by on Highway 18.

The access road to Lake arrowhead was rougher than Highway 18 but I succeeded in making it to the Arrowhead lodge. Not being hungry, thirsty or having to pee, I didn't go in. It looked like a dump anyway. Instead, I followed a dirt road with a sign beside it with an arrow pointing at the sky, announcing, "NORTH SHORE." I leaned forward and looked up in the sky through my windshield.

The Brat: " What are you doing? Do you think the north shore is hovering up there about ten thousand feet? What an idiot."

As I drove around to the north shore with the blue waters of the lake to my left, I made some conclusions about the development of Lake Arrowhead. It appeared to be a community that had started with high hopes but had deteriorated badly. Some of the cabins were spacious and well designed but were mostly in ill repair, with overgrown vegetation and peeling paint. After a frustrating twenty-minutes, I finally found Yosemite Drive and followed it to its dead end.

I was confronted with a solid wall of Spruce trees all about forty feet tall. Then I noticed fresh tire tracks leading to a space between two of the trees. I guessed that an overgrown limb from one of the spruce trees acted as kind of a secret door covering the access road to the Perkins Family's Idyllic mountain retreat.

If I had been in my Oldsmobile, I would have cut back the limb before driving my new car through there. I decided, however, that anything the limb could do to the Hudson's paint job would only be an improvement, so I gunned my motor and drove through. One had to be speaking figuratively to call the access to Charley's cabin a road. Compared to it, Highway eighteen was the Autobahn. I had to ease along, in first gear over rocks and limbs and all kinds of other shit. But finally, I spotted a tumbledown shack through the trees to my right. It was gloomy and eerie under the shade of trees growing too close together. I stopped my car, shut off the motor and got out.

Seeing no sign that there was anyone around, I limped toward the teetering structure, careful not to trip on fallen branches and rocks. The boards of its walls were weathered a silver color and green mold grew an inch thick on the cedar shake roof. The structure learned about thirty degrees to the west and It looked like the addition of a bird's nest would send the whole thing tumbling down to the forest floor, never to rise again. The shack was also tiny, no more than a couple of hundred square feet. I walked around behind the ramshackle structure and discovered a 1934 Ford pickup truck painted blue. The plate was covered with mud, so I took a handful of leaves and cleaned it off until I could read the number. It was 38M227, confirming that the truck was the one that belonged to Wade Perkins.

I made my way back around to the shack's open door. I could see door nailed together from boards leaning against the wall beside the opening. There were remnants of leather hinges nailed at three places along one edge but they were covered with green mold and had rotted away. Stooping down, I went inside. There were two rooms, one small, the other a little bigger. Inside the bigger room was a green canvas knapsack sitting on the dirt floor. Alongside it was a cardboard box containing some canned goods. In the center of the floor, someone had constructed a fire ring or stones that held the ashes of a fire. I bent down a felt the ashes, they were still warm. A few feet away from the fire ring, I saw a pallet laid out on the dirt. It consisted of a mattress of spruce boughs covered by a blanket, with two more blankets to cover up with. There being only one pallet, I guessed that Neither Carmen nor Wade had suffered from the cold at night. Naked bodies pressed together are seldom cold.

I backed out of the shack and headed toward my car wondering where the two kids were. I got my answer when I was halfway to my Hudson. I heard a crack like a hand being slammed down on a table hard and a small-caliber bullet struck a tree a foot away from my head. I turned toward the sound, put my hands up and waited.

Wade emerged from behind some bushes first, with Carmen following behind like a baby deer walking toward a stream. Wade was nervous and his right hand holding a Colt Woodsman .22 pistol was shaking. He was dressed in jeans, work boots, and a brown leather jacket. Carmen looked bedraggled, with her hair in wild tangles and wearing a dirty blue dress, some kind of moccasins and a tan sweater that was pulled tightly around her.

172 | D . W .   D R A K E

"Carmen," I said, "my name is Matt Cole. I'm a private investigator. I was hired by your brother Tony to find you and bring you home."

"T-Tony?" Carmen stammered.

"And Wade, I promised your mom that I would get you safely home too."

"How do I know that you are who you say you are?" asked Wade, still pointing the gun at me.

"You don't, but I have a gun much bigger than yours. If I wanted to do you harm, I would have come here in a different way, and you would be laid out now with smoking a hole between your eyes. Your father gave me the tip about where to find you. Do you think he would do that if I meant to hurt you?" I asked."

"I guess not," said Wade who lowered the gun and tucked it in his waistband.

The Brat: "What is the deal with people shoving the barrels of loaded guns down the front of their pants lately? It's like they want to shoot off their balls."

Carmen sidled up to Wade and he put a protective arm around her. They both looked at me with expectation. I limped over to my car, retrieved my bourbon bottle and held it up. "Anybody need a drink?" I asked. Wade shook his head stoically but Carmen rushed over and snatched the bottle from my hand sneaky quick, like a monkey snatching a cookie from a zoo attendant's pocket. She raised the bottle to her lips and took a healthy swig, then hugged the bourbon to her body, like she wanted to keep it. The two of us conducted a minor tug of war, but I won and got my bottle back. I glared at her for a second or two. Carmen looked at my face. I think she finally understood that if she really wanted to end up in worse trouble, she should make another grab for my whiskey bottle.

The Brat: "What about me? You're always forgetting about me."

I took a long pull on the bourbon just to please The Brat, recorked the bottle and put it back in the car.

Carmen abruptly sat down on the ground and started to cry. Wade squatted down beside the weeping girl and put his arms around her.

"Mister, I'm so scared. What are we gonna do?" said Carmen between sobs.

"First things first, My name is Matt and I'm going to get you out of this mess. How have you two been eating? Are you hungry?"

"Not too well," responded Wade. "We ate our last can of pork and beans this morning for breakfast."

Well, I need to go down to that lodge and make a phone call. While I'm there I'll pick up some food and bring it back. Wade, I'm going to take your truck, just in case I was followed up here, the bad guys won't know it. So hand over the keys," I said.

Wade reached in his jacket pocket and tossed me a key ring with two keys on it. I looked at the dial on my watch. It was almost two-thirty in the afternoon.

"While I'm gone, you two hide in that gully over there. If anyone other than me shows up, blast them. Let's trade guns."

I gave Wade my .38 Super-automatic with two extra clips of ammunition. And took his Woodsman in return.

"My Colt works just like your .22 pistol, only bigger and more powerful. If you have to use it on anybody, aim for the chest and keep shooting until the guy you're shooting at goes down before shooting at anyone else. Be careful, my gun is ready to fire, so don't go waving it around," I said. I made no mention of his chances of remaining alive in a gun battle with Siegel's goons.

Wade's truck drove surprisingly well on my trip to the lodge. It seemed to negotiate the rough road better than my car. When I reached the lodge and walked in the lobby I confirmed my initial assessment of the place as a dump. I've seen cleaner hotels on skid

-row. The café portion on the ground floor wasn't any cleaner than the rest of the lobby, but beggars can't be choosers. I ordered a bunch of hamburgers, fried potatoes and bottles of Coca-Cola to take out. While the food was being prepared I took my rolls of coins out of my pocket and stepped into the phonebooth in the lobby of the lodge to make a long-distance phone call. Connecting the call took a little time, much longer than the actual call. At any rate, the food was packaged and ready when I stepped out of the phonebooth. I retraced my route back up to the Perkin's cabin. Nobody had looked at me funny and I was pretty certain nobody had followed me back. When I drove up to the cabin I was vigorously waving my left arm out the window of the truck and shouting, "IT'S ME!" I didn't want a trigger happy Wade Perkins to mistake me for a bad guy.

The two young people snatched up the greasy hamburgers like Dr. Fate falling on a pack of Egyptian monsters. Every once in awhile they would pause in their feasting to take sips from small, thick glass bottles of Coca-Cola. Finally, their hunger sated, they sat arm in arm on the running boards of my Hudson.

CHAPTER SIXTEEN

LAKE ARROWHEAD
JUNE 19,1947
THURSDAY
1:00 P.M.

"Carmen," I said, "I want you to start from the beginning and tell me about your involvement with Ben Siegel."

Carmen took a deep breath, expelled it, then looked away for a moment while she gathered her thoughts. Then she began to speak. The timbre of her voice was high pitched and together with her New Jersey accent, it made her sound like one of the title characters in the Disney movie, "Snow White and the Seven Dwarfs." And I'm not talking about Snow White.

"A while back I began to get tired of my mother in New Jersey treating me like a child." She pronounced the last word as "choild." "She was always running my life. She told me where to go and who I could see. I got so sick of it I called my brother

Tony in Las Vegas and asked him if I could come out there and stay with him for a while."

The Brat: "At first, I thought she sounded like 'Sleepy,' but the more she talks I think she's definitely 'Sneezy.'"

"I met Ben Siegel one day in the casino at the Flamingo Hotel," continued Carmen. "Tony had gotten me a job there as a cigarette girl. Ben came up to me and he was so handsome and charming. He said, 'Hey beautiful, how about going out with me tonight, that is, if your husband approves.' I laughed and said back, 'Why Mr. Siegel, I don't have a husband." He said 'Even better. Meet me here at eight.' He took me to the hotel lounge that night and got me drunk. I woke up the next morning in his bed. I saw him regularly after that. I thought I was in love with him."

At this point, Carmen turned to Wade with big cow eyes. "I was a stupid, immature girl then," she said. " I know now that I wasn't truly in love with him at all. Our love is so much deeper than that, and will last forever."

The Brat: "It's always entertaining to listen to a female try to explain to boyfriend number 562 why it wasn't her fault at all that she enthusiastically allowed herself to be screwed by boyfriend number 561 in all the positions described in the Kama Sutra."

Captain Straight: "Shut up you, we don't need any of your sass right now."

"Carmen, Tell me about why you came to Los Angeles and what happened to you there," I prompted. At the rate she was going I'd be an old man before she finished.

"Ben told me one day that he wanted me to move to Los Angeles with him and be his appointment secretary. I jumped at the chance to do something for the man I thought I loved. One weekend he took me to L.A. on his chartered plane. I ended up in a room over that Virginia Hill bitch's garage. Every time I would see her she would call me a 'whore or a 'slut.' I was so unhappy."

"I had been cooped up in that tiny room for about a week when one night, Ben walked in my room without knocking. He pulled out his 'thing' and said. 'Suck this bitch." I told him, no, I wasn't gonna do it and he slapped me to the floor and kicked me. He told me if I didn't suck him he would kick me until I did. So I said to myself, Cahmen, I said, you're gonna have to do it. I finally did it but I didn't want to. He left after that. Every weekend after that it was the same thing. He didn't want to have sex with me, just for me to do the other thing. One time, a few days before I ran away I told him I wanted to go home to New Jersey. He beat me with his fists so bad it was hard to breathe afterwards. I slipped into the house the next day and called my Brother Tony. He told me to get out of there. But I couldn't do it, I had no money. I was so unhappy I thought about killing myself. Before this, I had met Wade. He was so nice to me and the only person around there who would talk to me. We fell in love, the real, deep kind, not what I thought I had with Ben."

"Why did you run away from the mansion. Was it just because Siegel was forcing you to give him oral sex?" I asked.

"No. One night I heard some banging and commotion in the garage below my room. Then I heard a sound like someone crying. I tiptoed out of my room and went downstairs into the backyard. I had on this blue dress I'm wearing now. I saw a light on in the garage and stuck my head around the edge of the door to see what was going on." said Carmen, and started to weep again. Tears flowed from her eyes like the stream from a medium-sized garden hose. I let her cry for a while before I asked her to continue. Finally, the tears abated and she continued, but with a look of terror on her face.

"Two of Ben's men were holding another man by his arms. The guy being held down was covered in blood. When I peeked around the corner, I saw Ben hit the guy with a stick or something and blood flew everywhere. I must have gasped or something because Ben and his guys looked over at me. I panicked. I ran through the back gate and down the alley for a few houses and then cut over to the street between two houses. I hid under a hedge and Ben's guys looked everywhere for me. I stayed there until it started to get light. After that, I went to the end of the block thinking I would go to a busy street and flag down a policeman. Then I saw Wade's truck coming down the street. I flagged him down and he drove me away from there. Wade told me he knew a safe place to hide and he brought me here."

"Did you recognize the man Ben was beating in the garage?" I asked.

"No, he was covered in so much blood that it could have been anybody."

"Which of Siegel's men were holding the man's arms while Ben worked him over?"

"One of them was the guy they call 'Vinnie,' Ben's main bodyguard. I didn't recognize the other one," replied Carmen.

"Okay, Just sit tight. In a few hours, we'll leave to take you back to your brother in Las Vegas. And Wade, I'll take you home tomorrow."

"Like hell, you will. As long as there's a threat to her, I'm not leaving," said Wade. They grabbed each other and their arms meshed like the jaws of a steam shovel."

"Wade and I are getting married when this is all over. Our love is so deep we can conquer anything as long as we're together. We'll love each other till the end of time," gushed Carmen.

The Brat: "Or, at least until the next guy comes along that tells her that her eyes are like two languid pools reflecting the languid light of a languid moon."

REQUIEM FOR BUGSY | 181

"Okay, we'll discuss all this with your brother Tony. For right now, let's concentrate on getting you safely to him," I said, tired of the conversation. I sat down behind the wheel of my car, rested my head against the seat and closed my eyes.

Captain Straight: "Since it wasn't Carmen who was murdered in that garage, It's a good bet it was Johnny Falcone after all. Those two guys who said they saw him alive in Chicago were either lying, or it was a case of mistaken identity."

The Brat: "No shit? Did you figure that out all by yourself or did a falling chunk of frozen piss from a passing airliner smack you in the head and improve your intelligence quotient?"

Captain Straight: I've had about enough of your mouth. You may think you're funny, but nobody else does. Try saying something constructive for once, you little bastard."

The Brat: "Now ordinarily if such words were spoken by two guys, there'd be a fistfight. But in case you haven't noticed, we have no fists to fight with. We're just figments of Matt's imagination."

"Guys, c'mon, give me a break and be quiet for a while," I said out loud, prompting a weird look from Wade Perkins.

We stayed at the cabin until a quarter to seven in the evening. I figured that would give us just enough time to get to Route 66 at San Bernardino before full dark. Finally, when I judged the time was right, I bundled Carmen and Wade into the back seat, told then to keep low and out of sight, and started out.

The Brat: "What a smell. Boy, are these two ripe. You'd think they'd have had the sense to find a stream to bathe in during their time up on this mountain. I think I'm gonna gag."

It was true, the stench was almost overpowering. I rolled down my window and adjusted my wind wing to blow outside air on my face. It lessened the smell somewhat. But the truth was, I had no choice but to try to ignore the reek of unwashed bodies. I took Highway 18 back down the mountain to San Bernardino. It was quiet in the car as well as my head for the first half of the mountain drive. Then The Brat spoke up.

The Brat: "I got that feeling again."

Captain Straight: "What now? What feeling?"

The Brat: "It's really a weird sensation. It's like I sense that someone has the crosshairs of a telescopic sight focused on the back of Matt's head."

Captain straight: "Forget it. You're just jumpy."

The thought of someone aiming a rifle at my cranium made me involuntarily reach up and rub the back of my head. But my head didn't explode in a gooey mess of gray brain matter and blood on the rest of the way down the mountain. The daylight was almost gone and the streetlights were winking on one by one when I turned right on Foothill and followed it for a short distance to the stop sign at Route 66. I turned right and headed north.

The engine of my old Hudson labored on the grade at Cajon Pass. Several times I had to downshift down into second to keep up any speed at all. But the traffic was light and thankfully, we didn't get stuck behind any trucks while climbing the grade. Once we came out on the plateau at the top of the pass, the old car's engine thanked me by surging forward. Though silent up to this point, Carmen then began to whine.

"I need to go to the bathroom. Can't we stop soon?"

The Brat: "Tell her to hold it."

"Hold it," I called over the seat.

"I can't hold it much longer and I'm hungry."

"Well, you're gonna have to hold it for a while. There's no place to stop right now.

"Mister whatever your name is, I'm hurting back here. If you don't stop soon, I'll tell Tony when I see him that you were mistreating me."

The Brat: "Tell me again why Tony Cardello wants to get this whining bitch back?"

"I'll stop after we get through Victorville. It's just a few more miles. I'll pull over and you can pee beside the car. I won't look," I said.

After I made the unscheduled stop and Carmen relieved herself, she still didn't stop complaining.

"I'm still hungry and thirsty and I'm sick of ducking down in the back of this car. Why can't we sit up and ride like normal people." Her little seven dwarf's voice had turned whiny and it grated on my nerves.

"Because half the gangsters in California are out searching for you to put a bullet in your head," I exploded. "Shut up and be quiet"

"I beg your pardon! People don't speak to me that way. I'm gonna tell my brother!"

The Brat: "Did you notice how quiet Wade has been back there? I'll bet he's learning all kinds of interesting shit about the personality of his sweet bride to be."

Carmen kept it up. By the time we neared Barstow, I was ready to tie her up, prop her up beside the road and put a sign around her neck telling Bugsy to come and get her. But I didn't.

And at the junction of US Route 66 and US Route 91, I pulled off the road and parked in one of the stalls of a drive-in restaurant. A sign advertised the place as, "DAN'S DRIVE-IN." Another sign hanging from the eaves of the roof announced: "THE ONLY CAR-HOP SERVICE BETWEEN HERE AND ALBUQUERQUE." Smelling as bad as my two passengers did, I didn't dare take them into a regular restaurant.

A teenaged girl in a bellhop's uniform with two vertical rows of silver buttons from waist to each shoulder, and a little pill hat, roller-skated up to my window. Before she could say anything she got a whiff through the open side window of Carmen and Wade, smelling like two halves of a three-day dead road-killed Moose. She wrinkled her nose and her eyes watered a little, but the youngster was game, I'll say that about her. In an instant, her smile was back and she wrote down our order on a little pad and skated away.

I just had a big paper cup of coffee, but Carmen and Wade ordered enough food to feed an entire Okie extended family, along with some extra "cousins" that no one knew where exactly to place in the family tree. The food was brought on metal trays that balanced on the window sills using short braces with rubber tips to protect the paint of the car. I genuinely hoped that if I could stuff Carmen full of enough food, she would shut the hell up for the rest of the trip.

CHAPTER SEVENTEEN

US ROUTE 91, SOUTH OF BAKER
JUNE 19, 1947
THURSDAY
9:15 P.M.

T he big meal didn't shut Carmen up for long. About forty miles past Barstow, she began to bitch again that she had to go to the bathroom.

"Again?" I exclaimed. "You're like a female cougar marking her territory. Are you trying to claim all of the California desert as 'Carmenland', or just a narrow strip on the side of the highway?"

"You're such a nasty man. I can't help it if I have to pee," replied Carmen, aka "Sneezy" the dwarf.

"Mister, I have to go really bad too," said Wade in a nervous voice.

"Little Matt: "The bladder just told me he's full up too. He said all his gauges are in the red.""

The Brat: "It's partly your fault, you know. You swilled all that coffee in Barstow."

"Alright!" I called over the seat. "I'll find a place for us all to piss. But this will be the last time I'm stopping before I dump you onto your brother's lap.""

After a mile or two I spotted a flat area of cleared desert on which someone had dumped enormous mounds of gravel and sand. It was ahead beside the highway on the right. I surmised that it was there to be used by highway work crews to maintain the road. After turning right into the area, I drove behind one of the mounds. I got out, leaving the motor running and the lights on, and stood beside my car on the driver's side. Wade took the passenger side and Carmen scurried away to find some privacy behind the next mound.

"Watch out for snakes," I called out to her, but she didn't acknowledge me.

I whipped Little Matt out and started to urinate while performing the universal male pissing ritual of hawking and spitting, and uttering a satisfied "Ahhh." It was too dark to perform the other part of the ritual, seeing how far I could project my stream.

I should have known better, a man is never more vulnerable than when he is pissing. Siegel's goons used my compromised position to their advantage and took us. To my everlasting chagrin, they made it look really easy.

Two cars came roaring in from the south with their lights off, and a car skidded to a stop on each side of my Hudson. One was a long black Chrysler and the other was a white Ford sedan. I was still holding Little Matt when a blinding light was shined in my face and I just knew that I had more ordinance pointed at me at that moment than possessed by the entire Third United States Army, including possibly General Patton's ivory-handled cowboy pistol. I tucked Little Matt away, zipped up and then stood very still.

Someone grabbed me from behind and slammed my face down on the hood of my Hudson and a hand deftly relieved me of my gun. A second later Wade's head was also mashed against the hood on the other side of the car. I didn't see what had happened to Carmen. I hoped she had hidden or ran off into the desert. My hopes were dashed when I heard her voice, "Let go of me. you're hurting me. I'm gonna tell my brother!"

Carmen, Wade and I were brought from different points and roughly made to sit together on the ground in the cone of light from the headlamps of my car. As they stood around us, I got a good look at all five of our assailants. I recognized one of the goons because I make it a habit to remember the faces of people who shove guns in my face. It was Vinnie Alfonsi, Siegel's head bodyguard, and he had a triumphant smirk on his pocked face. The other four guys looked like cast members from an Edward G. Robinson gangster movie. They all looked identical. I began to wonder if in some secret location, maybe on the far side of the moon, there was a mafia torpedo factory run by a mad scientist, cranking out gangster goons around the clock. I speculated whether they all had tags sewn into the folds on the back of their necks like mattresses.

The Brat: "Well slick, these guys made you look like an amateur. You didn't even draw your gun!"

I sat there beating up on myself for getting Carmen and Wade in this situation. After all, I told them I would protect them. I figured the next step would be a bullet in the back of each of our heads. But I was wrong. Vinnie didn't order us killed on the spot. Apparently, he had something else in mind.

"Tie that asshole up and put him in the trunk of the Chrysler," said Vinnie to two of the goons. He was pointing with his revolver at Wade. "Then cuff the girl an' the gumshoe together and put 'em in the back seat."

I was roughly jerked to my feet and soon found myself with my right wrist handcuffed to Carmen's left and sitting on the back seat of the Chrysler. One of the gangsters was perched on the jump seat opposite me pointing a .32 auto pistol at my head. Through the rear window of the big car, I heard Vinnie semi-shouting instructions to two of his troops.

"You two take the Ford and get back to L.A. You just have enough time to make it back to the mansion. The boss is flyin' in at four. Oh, and before you go, take that old heap and hide it further in away from the road behind one a these piles a sand. Throw the keys out into the desert."

Vinnie got in the front passenger seat of the Chrysler and slammed the door. The driver gunned the motor, drove out onto Route 91 and headed north. The car hadn't traveled a mile before Carmen started to whine again.

"I didn't get a chance to pee back there. I gotta go real bad now."

The Brat: "It'll almost be worth getting executed to see that whiny bitch get hers first."

"Shut up!" shouted Vinnie. "Just hold it. But if you piss all over my back seat, I'll have to kill you twice."

"If I do pee on your seat, it'll be your fault," retorted Carmen.

Vinnie turned in the front seat, looked back and gave Carmen a withering look. "Look, Bitch, if you don't shut the hell up, I'll drill you right here."

"Threatening her isn't going to work. I already tried, nothing works," I interjected.

"EVERYBODY SHUT THE FUCK UP!" yelled Vinnie. "Georgie, stop beside the road."

When the car stopped, Vinnie got out, yanked open the rear door and jerked Carmen out of the rear seat. Because of the handcuffs, I was sprawled half in and half out of the door. Carmen gratefully pulled down her panties and squatted there in plain sight, thereby adding a whole new territory to Carmenland.

We blew through Baker without stopping. By that time Carmen hadn't complained about anything for a least twenty miles. Vinnie's mood took on a change and he got talkative.

Contrary to what you see in Hollywood gangster movies or hear on the radio, mob killers almost never have long conversations with their victims before shooting them. The reason for this is that the killers usually don't know their victims, and aren't emotionally involved with them. They would tell you that they're just performing a necessary service for pay, like an auto mechanic or a grocery clerk. Their favorite method of operation is to approach their victim unawares and put a bullet in the back of his or her head without saying anything. Vinnie Alfonsi turned out to be the exception to the rule.

"I bet you're wonderin' how we got on to you, aren't you gumshoe," began Vinnie. He was sitting sideways in his seat and looking back at me with an evil grin. "A friend of ours in the phone company put a tap on your office phone. When that guy

Perkins called in and said he wanted to talk to you, he gave his address to your girl on the phone. We staked out his address until you got there an' then we tailed you till you found the bitch and her boyfriend."

"Georgie here is a whiz at tailin' guys. And we used two cars to tail you and talked to each other with this," said Vinnie, and held up an olive-drab colored, army Walkie-talkie. "We bought a pair a these from a army surplus store."

As we were crossing the Nevada border, my long-time companions inside my head began to speculate on our ultimate destination.

Captain Straight: "Do you suppose they're taking us directly to Bugsy Siegel in Las Vegas?"

The Brat: "Could be. We'll know soon enough. What I don't understand is why Vinnie didn't just do us all in back where they first grabbed us. Three quick bullets to the head and this is all over."

Captain Straight: "I think Vinnie must have orders not to leave any bodies lying around. That's the only explanation that makes sense. Of course, they could have shot Matt, Carmen, and Wade behind those sand piles and put the bodies in their cars and transported them to the dumping place. But transporting bodies leaking blood is messy and hard to clean and leaves evidence behind for the cops to find."

I wanted to tell them to stop discussing my demise, in the same manner, they would discuss the relative merits of Russian and Jewish rye bread. But I couldn't yell out for them to shut the hell up for obvious reasons.

"I'm cold. The night air is blowing right on me. Can you roll up your window a little bit?" Carmen asked Vinnie.

'Shut up Bitch!" replied Vinnie.

"If you had let me get my sweater from the other car, I wouldn't be so cold. It's your fault."

"I got the window down cause you smell like a dead cow that's been rottin' in the sun for a week. Don't worry, you won't be cold for much longer," replied Vinnie.

The Brat: "You know, Tony Cardello saying his sister wasn't too bright was the understatement of the century, on a par with calling the storming of Iwo Jima an invigorating morning excursion. This moron has no conception of what Vinnie has in store for her."

About ten miles outside Las Vegas, Georgie slowed down and made a left turn onto a dirt road. For about three or four miles we bumped along a rough road passing big boulders and sagebrush. Then Georgia veered to the left and shortly I saw that we were driving up into a canyon with steep rock walls on both sides. The car stopped at the head of the canyon and the headlights illuminated a curious structure. Perched on a level spot up the sloping canyon wall, and illuminated by the headlights of the Chrysler, was what Looked like the top of an old fashioned well, only much bigger. There was a heavy timber crossbar suspended between two braced posts. In the middle of the crossbar, there was a suspended pulley with a rope looped over it and running straight down.

"Okay kiddies, all out. We're here," said Vinnie.

'Do you want the guy in the trunk out too?" asked Georgie.

"Nah, we'll do him last, after we take care of the other two, " replied Vinnie.

Carmen and I were jerked out of the car as a unit and walked across sand and gravel toward the structure. As we got closer, I saw that the rope suspended from the pulley didn't stop at the ground but kept going down a dark hole about four feet wide.

CHAPTER EIGHTEEN

NEVADA DESERT SOUTH OF LAS VEGAS
JUNE 19, 1947
THURSDAY
10:30 P.M.

66 **I**t's an old mine shaft. It's a thousand feet deep, give or take a few feet," said Vinnie smiling. "so you'll have time to make peace with your maker on the way down. If you're not a prayin' man, you can talk to the bitch on the way down for all I care."

I looked around desperately. But I saw resistance was useless. The silent gangster who had covered me in the back seat had exchanged his .32 auto for a pump shotgun, which he now had pointed at my belly button. Carmen, who had been silent for the last few minutes, suddenly whirled to face Vinnie.

"You're not gonna throw me in there you asshole," she spat.

Vinnie backhanded her hard. Carmen fell back and came to rest against my shins.

"Get up Bitch," said Vinnie.

"Hit her again Vinnie, and you're going to wish you didn't," I told him.

"Who's gonna make me wish I didn't? You?" replied Vinnie, looking smug.

"No, not me," I replied, "but the five guys I hired to tail you as you tailed me from San Bernardino."

"Gumshoe, that's the oldest trick in the book. Do you really think I'll be fooled by something like that?" said Vinnie, who then raised his voice.

" WHOEVER YOU ARE OUT THERE, YOU SHOULD PROBABLY SHOOT VERN HERE," he yelled, pointing at the hood with the scattergun. "HE HAS THE SHOTGUN!" continued Vinnie and chuckled.

Suddenly, there was a muzzle flash on the other side of the Chrysler and a shot echoed around the canyon. The head of Vern the gangster holding the shotgun exploded and he crumpled to the ground like a little girl's rag doll. Georgie, Vinnie's expert shadower, tried to pull a .38 revolver from his shoulder holster. But his luck was no better than the hood with the shotgun. Another shot rang out. And a rapidly spreading red stain appeared on the front of Georgie's suit. He toppled over backward, the heels of his shoes drummed on the ground for a few moments, and then he was still.

Vinnie stood there frozen like a statue as a voice boomed out of the dark behind the Chrysler.

"Vinnie, Be very still old friend, or you'll join the others. Peeper, circle around behind him and get his gun. Don't get in my line of sight."

I did what I was told, dragging Carmen with me. I frisked Vinnie, took my own gun from his waistband, as well as his .38 revolver. After I had him covered with my gun, I fished around in his pants pockets until I found the keys to the handcuffs. Quickly, I unlocked the cuffs and removed them from Carmen's and my wrists and snapped them on Vinnie's wrists behind his back. Lastly, as a precaution, I gathered up three handguns and a shotgun and tossed them down the mineshaft. People who leave loaded guns just lying around often live to regret it. When this was done, I yelled out, "CLEAR."

The giant bulk of Carlo the mountain and a half slowly lumbered out of the darkness and into the light. He was carrying a lever-action rifle in one of his huge hands. Either Carlo had shown remarkable forethought in bringing the rifle, or he happened the meet a masked man and his Indian companion back in the canyon somewhere and Tonto loaned him his spare Winchester.

"About fucking time, Carlo," I said. " Why didn't you take these assholes when they first jumped us.?"

"Your welcome Peeper. But there were too many of them then. I had to wait."

"Cousin Carlo!" shouted Carmen with glee, ran to him and hugged him. "How come you're here?"

"The Peeper here called me at Virginia's mansion before you left Lake Arrowhead. He was pretty sure he was bein' tailed. He wanted me to tail the tailers and act as an insurance policy in case somethin' like this happened. I been behind you ever since Barstow."

All through this conversation, Vinnie Alfonsi stood in the same place trembling. I could see his Adam's apple bobbing up and down as he swallowed repeatedly with nervousness. He eyed us with trepidation as we walked up to him. A dark stain began to spread down the leg of his suit from his groin.

"Hey Carlo, old pal, I would'na done all this if I knew this gal was your cousin," croaked out Vinnie.

"Vinnie, Why did Siegel want to kill Carmen so bad?" I asked.

"Cause she saw him beatin' on Johnny Falcone."

"So Ben Siegel killed Johnny Falcone."

"Yeah," said Vinnie. "But he really din mean ta kill him. All he intended ta do was rough him up a little bit. But Ben went crazy and beat him to death with an iron bar. It all started when the boss went to a cocktail party at George Raft's house. A bunch of Hollywood stars were there. Johnny Falcone also turned up at the party, already drunk. I don't know if he was invited or just showed up, but Johnny starts raggin' on the boss an' started makin' jokes about the boss's nickname bein' 'Bugsy.' He said the boss was nicknamed 'Bugsy" cause he was a crazy bastard. Frank Sinatra laughed. Cary Grant laughed. Even George Raft laughed. But the boss didn't laugh. He told us, his bodyguards, to waylay Johnny on his way home with covered faces an' blindfold him an' take him to the garage at the mansion an' work him over for a while. Johnny was such an arrogant little shit, who thought he was untouchable cause he was Jack Dragna's nephew. So he never had bodyguards go around with him."

"So we followed Johnny from the party and snatched him at a stoplight. We blindfolded him and took him to the garage at Virginia's house and began to work him over, but only in the stomach where the bruises wouldn't show. Johnny turned out to be just as tough as his mouth. He kept yelling that Ben Siegel was a crazy yellow bastard who sent boys to do a man's work. The boss, who was listenin' outside of the garage all of a sudden come rushin' in with an iron bar and start hitting Johnny Falcone. He wouldn't stop no matter how hard we tried to stop him. Then that dizzy dame Carmen showed up at the door and saw the boss covered in Johnny's blood. Before we could grab her, she ran away. We looked all over the neighborhood for her but she was in the wind. Afterwards we dumped Johnny's body in Santa Monica Bay, weighed down with a chain. The boss told us to find Carmen and get rid of her cause a what she seen. When the gumshoe started sniffin' round the garage an' snitched us off to Dragna's people, the boss said to take care of him too. Carlo, we been friends for years. I was only doin what the boss told me to do. You let me go an I'll get outa town an you'll never see me again."

Carlo looked Vinnie in the eye. But this was a different Carlo from the one I knew. Gone was the supposed dim-witted amiable giant. In its place was a stern-faced colossus, with angry eyes that flashed at his former colleague.

"I sympathize with you, Vinnie. I really do. I know that you were only doin' what you were told to do," said Carlo softly. He suddenly grabbed the front of Vinnie's suit, lifted him off the ground with one arm and brought his face within inches of his own.

"But you hit Carmen and she's my cousin. She's family. And you of all people should know how Sicilians feel about family," said Carlo, and tossed Vinnie into the gaping maw of the mineshaft as easily as throwing away a cigarette butt. The would-be killer screamed all the way down the shaft. Starting off strong and blood curdling, his screams got fainter and fainter the farther he fell down the shaft until we heard a muted thud, and he wasn't screaming anymore.

Carlo then walked over to the two mobsters he has shot. He picked one up in each of his massive hands, walked over to the mouth of the mineshaft and tossed them in.

The Brat: "Attention happy campers. When departing your campsite, please pick up all your trash and place it in the appropriate receptacle."

"We better get Wade out of the trunk before he suffocates," I told Carlo and he nodded. When I opened the trunk lid, Wade was lying there bound and gagged and wild-eyed. I borrowed a small penknife from Carlo, severed the ropes that held him and helped him out of the trunk.

"Wade, my darling," said Carmen. She ran to the young man and embraced him. Wade Perkins, for his part, was giving Carmen that peculiar look (you husbands know the one I'm talking about) that men don't typically give their wives until about ten or fifteen years after the wedding.

Wade was gaping at Carlo. "Who is he? And where are those other guys that put me in that trunk?"

"They're gone," I replied. "Carlo here showed up and asked them politely to let us go and they did."

"But I heard shooting. What was that all about?"

"Oh, that was nothing," I explained. "One of the guys that kidnapped us dared Carlo to shoot a tin can off the top of his head at forty feet. Unfortunately, Carlo shot a little low. But it's okay, he only grazed the guy and a band-aid fixed him right up. Then we all stood around talking about the good old times everyone had during prohibition and the Saint Valentine's day massacre. After a while, the other guys excused themselves, saying that they had another kidnapping scheduled and had to go." I could see that Wade was very skeptical of my explanation, but he didn't say anything more.

"I'm cold and I'm thirsty and I need to pee again," announced Carmen.

The Brat: "That mineshaft isn't near to being full of bodies yet. There's plenty of room for one more."

"We need to get out of here and get Carmen to Tony as soon as we can. She's a delightful young lady but I've had about as much of her company as I can stand for one lifetime," I said while walking toward the Chrysler.

Carlo stopped me. "We can't use that car. It's too well known around Las Vegas. We'll take mine. It's parked just around the last bend in the canyon."

As the four of us trudged down the canyon floor toward Carlo's car, the giant signaled to me to hold back. He wanted to speak to me privately. When Carmen and Wade were out of earshot, he turned his massive head toward me.

"In my line of work, and especially with the people I work around now, it's very advantageous for me to appear to be just a big, dumb ox, without a brain in my head. How this act benefits me is none of your business, but trust me, it does. I let the mask slip a couple of times with you, so I know you've figured out my secret. I would be very displeased with you if you were to tell anyone about my deception, especially my cousin Tony. Bad things have been known to happen to people I'm displeased with, nuff said?"

"Nuff said," I replied.

Carlo's car turned out to be a 1946 maroon Buick sedan. We all piled in and drove back to the blacktop of Route 91, then he turned north, toward Las Vegas. At the first phone booth we passed after entering the town of Las Vegas, Carlo stopped and made a phone call. I assumed it was to Tony Cardello. He came back to the car from the phonebooth and sat stoically behind the wheel of his car, saying nothing.

"I'm hot. Can you roll down the windows, and I still have to pee," said Carmen in her "Sneezy" voice. Carlo ignored her. After about twenty minutes, the phone in the booth started to ring and

Carlo went to answer it. He came back to the car, started it up and drove away.

We ended up at the Golden Nugget Hotel on Fremont street. The place looked brand new like it had just been built. We didn't go in the front entrance but circled around to Carson Avenue, where Carlo parked his Buick and we went in the rear entrance of the hotel. Taking the back stairs to the third floor, the four of us walked along a carpeted hallway and stopped at room 315, and Carlo knocked on the wood door.

The door was answered by a flashy looking blonde woman in her late thirties. She didn't smile as she backed away to allow us to enter. Standing across the room, by the bed, was Tony Cardello.

"Tony!" shouted Carmen and rushed into his arms. After a moment she pushed away from her brother and pointed her right index finger at me. "That man didn't treat me nice. He wouldn't let me go pee or anything. I think you should beat him up!"

Tony looked down at his sister's face. "Carmen, that guy is the reason you're still alive," he said and then stopped and wrinkled his nose. "Carmen, that stink, what have you been doing? Rolling in pig shit?"

"It's not my fault Tony. It's that guy's fault," she said pointing at me again. "He was in such a hurry, he wouldn't let me stop and take a bath or eat or anything."

"Who is this guy?" asked Tony, pointing at Wade.

"That's Wade, the man I love. Out love is a towering love that will last all through all eternity. We want to get married," replied Carmen.

"Uh-huh," said Tony, then turned to the blonde woman who had answered the door.

"Sylvia, Take Carmen to the room next door and clean her up. There are soap and towels and women's stuff in the bathroom. When the two females had disappeared through a connecting door into the next room, Tony's gaze fell on Wade.

"Well Wade here's the deal. Carmen is going out of the country for a while. Maybe for a couple of years. She's going to stay with relatives in the old country until I think it's safe for her to return. Carmen will I'm sure be in and out of love with eight or ten new guys by then, including probably the village priest. But if you two still love each other when she returns, then we'll talk about marriage. But in the meantime, if you breathe a word about any of this to anyone, especially the newspapers, the cops or the feds, I'll come after you. And not just you but also your folk's and all your relatives."

The Brat: "Not to mention, your boy scout leader when you were twelve, all your high school girlfriends and your pet parakeet."

"Do you understand me?" asked Tony.

"Yessir," stammered Wade bobbing his head up and down enthusiastically. Tony took some money from his pocket and pressed it into Wade's hand.

"There's enough there to get a train ticket back to Los Angeles and for cab fare home from Union station. The Las Vegas train station is two blocks west from the front door of this hotel. Now blow, " said Tony menacingly. Wade was out the door like a V-2 rocket taking off for London.

When he was gone Tony sat down on the hotel bed. Carlo stood with his arms folded near the connecting door.

"I don't think You'll see Wade Perkins ever again. I think this trip has been an eye-opener for him regarding Carmen. If it comes to a choice between joining the French Foreign Legion and marrying Carmen, I think he'll be memorizing a book of French phrases and trying to grow one of those little thin mustaches," I said.

"Never mind that now," said Tony. "We got ourselves a big problem.

CHAPTER NINETEEN

LAS VEGAS
JUNE 20, 1947
FRIDAY
12:30 A.M.

"**P**eeper, go on down to the hotel bar," said Tony Cardello. "You look like you need a drink real bad. Carlo and I have to have a talk and I don't want you to be butting in with a bunch of wisecracks."

The Brat: "Finally! Somebody has come up with an intelligent suggestion. I think I'm going to have to revise upward my opinion of Tony."

As I walked into the bar, some of the patrons looked at me askance because of my rumpled khaki work clothes and blue ball cap. But they soon lost interest in me and the bartender didn't care if I was naked as long as I had money sitting on the bar. I got reacquainted with my friend Jack Daniel's. It was a tearful reunion, with plenty of hugs and kisses. Old Jack and I declared our undying love for each other for about the ten thousandth time. I told him if any of those smart-assed Yankee revenuers ever come down to Tennessee and mess with him, to call me right away and I would hop a train down south and help him fight them off. With the first swallow of the smooth amber bourbon whiskey, I began to relax. By the fourth glass, I was so relaxed, I was ready to go night-night.

Then Carlo walked into the bar, crooked a finger at me, and spoiled all the fun. He then turned and rumbled toward the elevator. I hurried after him, well, as much as a man can hurry with a gimpy left leg.

Back in the hotel room upstairs, Tony gave me an annoyed look. I was standing near the foot of the bed weaving like a flagpole with a loose base being buffeted by the wind. "Damn Peeper, I said have a drink, not a whole fucking barrel," he said

"I came. I saw. I conquered," I said, only slurring my words a wee bit.

"Well, what I have to tell you will sober you up pretty quick. Peeper, Ben Siegel hasn't got as far as he has in the rackets by being stupid. Add to that, he's as cunning as a cobra. When Vinnie and his boys fail to show up or call in by Monday, he'll start putting two and two together. He'll know that somebody took Vinnie and his boys out of the picture and wonder who did it. The trail of breadcrumbs will eventually lead back to me and Carlo" said Tony.

I stood there nodding my head stupidly. Through the alcoholic haze, I began to get an inkling of where this conversation was headed and I didn't like it.

"If we don't act now," continued Tony, "we'll all probably be dead before Monday night. I know it sounds crazy, but we have to kill Ben Siegel as soon as possible, and do it in a way that nobody knows we were the ones who did it."

Tony had been right. The words he uttered did have the effect of sobering me up. I went from pleasantly drunk to full-blown, sober panic without stopping at any of the stations in between. I sat down on the bed in shock, with my mouth gaping open.

Captain Straight: "That's it, brother, I'm going to find myself somebody else's head to occupy."

"Just to clarify, you want me, who is not a certified member of the mob, and who has not gone through the hitman training course at Al Capone U, to help you assassinate Bugsy Siegel?"

The Brat: "Ask him if you can just sit in your apartment and think positive thoughts while the murder is happening."

"Can't I just sit in my apartment and think positive thoughts while you hit Bugsy? I'm very good at giving moral support." I said. Tony didn't dignify my response with an answer. Instead, he turned toward Carlo.

"Carlo, do you think that when I tipped off the peeper here about the hit team that was on its way to his office, was I doing him a favor?"

"Yeah, Tony. It was a thing a true friend would do," replied Carlo.

"And, do you think the peeper here realizes that just because Vinnie and his boys are dead that he's not off the hook, and that Ben Siegel will just keep sending other guys until both he and Carmen are dead," asked Tony.

"No Tony, I don't think he realizes that," replied Carlo.

"Okay, okay, What will my role in this assassination be?" I asked.

"Carlo and I will do the actual hit. Your job will be to have your car nearby with the motor running in case everything turns to shit and we have to make a hasty exit out of Virginia Hill's mansion," replied Tony.

"So I will only be the getaway driver?" I asked.

"Yeah, and only if Carlo and I screw the pooch inside the mansion. If everything goes well, you'll be able to drive away and go about your business as if nothing had happened," said Tony.

"Okay," I said.

"See, that wasn't so bad," said Tony, like he had pulled one of my teeth, and not like he had just enrolled me in an assassination plot against probably the most dangerous man in North America.

"Okay listen up," said Tony. " Ben called me into his office today. He said Vinnie and his regular bodyguards were out doing a little job for him. He said I was to organize a security squad from the guys at the hotel and go with him to L.A. for the weekend. I picked the worst shots I could find to be on the detail. We're leaving by plane at two-thirty A.M., about an hour from now. Ben is going out to dinner tonight at a fancy restaurant with a guy named Alan Smiley, Chick Hill and Chick's girlfriend. When they get back to the mansion, we wait until Ben is alone somewhere and I come up behind him and put a bullet in the back of his head. Afterward, I'll tell a bullshit story about seeing a guy dressed all in black, escaping from a window with a gun in his hand. Carlo, if I blow it and the whole thing all turns to shit, you will have to take out the rest of the guards. You'll have to act fast and pop them all in the head real quick. Peeper, you wait for five minutes after you hear shots from inside the mansion. If we don't come by then, we're not coming. Then you high-tail it out of there before the cops show up. Any questions?"

"Hey wait a minute," I protested. "That's it? That's all the planning? Carlo is supposed to shoot four or five guys in the head, just like that? What happens if he misses one and gets plugged himself. No, I think we should talk about this some more."

"Then I come barreling out the front door leaving Carlo in a pool of blood, jump in your car and we get out of there. Look, Peeper, no plan is perfect but the best ones are simple. Carlo, you need to get back to the mansion asap. What did you tell them when you left to go help the peeper?" asked Tony.

"I told Solly I had the shits. I said I was going to see a doctor and I would be back as soon as I could," replied Carlo.

Tony nodded, then told Carlo. "Take the Peeper back to his car on your way to L.A. And you Peeper, after dark tonight, park your car down the street from the mansion. When you see Siegel return from the restaurant in his Cadillac about nine-thirty or ten, pull up close to the house and be ready with the motor running."

Carlo's Buick was silent as he drove me south from Las Vegas. Neither one of us felt like talking. I was anxious to see if my Hudson was still where Vinnie's helper had parked it. If it was gone, I guessed I would have to buy another used car in Los Angeles. But we got lucky. It was parked behind the piles of sand and gravel just where the gangster had left it, but the leys weren't in it.

Instead of hot wiring my car right off, I borrowed a flashlight from Carlo and scanned the desert behind the car. At first, all I saw was ghostly looking sagebrush and empty space. Then, in the light of the beam from the flashlight, I saw a reflection from a bush about twenty feet out in the desert. I limped across the uneven ground and found my keyring with its two keys, hanging from a branch of the bush. When one of my kidnappers had thrown the keys away, he had only made a halfhearted throw. I went back to where Carlo was waiting and handed him back his flashlight.

Carlo extended his huge right paw through the open window. "Peeper, If everything goes right tonight, this is the last time we will be seeing each other. Take care of yourself, and thanks for saving Carmen. I know she's a pain in the ass, but she's family and that's what counts."

I shook his bear paw but didn't say anything in return, I just nodded my head. He backed up his car, made a looping turn and headed south on Route 91.

The Brat: "So Matthew Cole, boy assassin, do you have any idea how much trouble you have gotten yourself into this time?"

I limped over to my Hudson, put the key in the ignition and hit the starter button on the dash. I was rewarded with a healthy roar as my faithful old chariot came to life. I took a last look around the area and then pulled out on the highway about three or four miles or so behind Carlo.

I arrived in the outskirts of Los Angeles about seven, Friday morning. I was bushed. I felt like I hadn't slept for a week. I found a diner and parked in a corner of its parking lot, got in the back seat of the Hudson and slept like a stone for three hours. When I awoke I felt worse than when I went to sleep. I staggered into the diner begging for coffee. After I drank the first cup I felt better. I yelled at the waitress for more. As the waitress carried a plate of pancakes to another table, I suddenly realized that I was famished. I ordered the biggest breakfast on the diner menu. A huge platter arrived laden with bacon, sausage patties, eggs, potatoes, and pancakes. I devoured every morsel like a pig and afterward, I felt better still.

As I left the diner I took stock of my situation. Dare I go to my apartment and get cleaned up? Ben Siegel had put Vinnie and his boys on my trail, but were there others waiting to pounce on me the minute I stepped into my apartment? I didn't think so. Siegel had a lot of gangsters working for him but they all had jobs in the rackets. He couldn't afford to take too many of his guys away from their jobs for very long. I decided that I would chance going to my apartment but be very careful about it.

I parked the Hudson a half-block west of my building and studied who went in and came out for fifteen minutes. I didn't see anybody loitering on the street or sitting in cars in the area. Next, I drove around to the alley in the rear and parked for another fifteen minutes. I didn't notice anyone suspicious. Of course, there might have been twenty hoods crouched inside my apartment just waiting to pounce when I turned the key in the lock, but there was no way to check that. I would just have to enter with my gun in my hand.

I parked my Hudson in the alley a block away and limped toward my building. My cap was pulled down, obscuring my face.

On the way, I passed a trash can. On top of it was a large cardboard box. I picked up the box, and carrying it high, covering the bottom part of my face, I entered my building. I was hoping that if there were any of Siegel's men loitering around that I hadn't seen, I would look to them like a handyman going in to repair something.

On my way across the empty lobby, I stopped at the mailboxes, put down the box on the floor and retrieved a stack of mail from my box. Taking the elevator up to my floor, I got off and approached my apartment door as quietly as I could. I drew my pistol and held my ear to the door listening for fifteen seconds. Not hearing anything, I reached for the doorknob and slowly turned it. The door was unlocked.

I entered my apartment hard and fast with my gun up and ready to shoot. There were no gangsters hiding inside and the place looked pretty much as I had last left it. The only signs that someone had made a hurried search was a knocked over pole lamp and a few of the bottles in my empty beer bottle collection had been knocked from their perch from the coffee table onto the rug. After checking the other rooms, I relocked the door.

Keeping my pistol handy, I stripped off my khaki work clothes and ballcap, luxuriated in a hot bath, washed my hair, brushed my teeth, and shaved. Feeling clean again, I dressed in my last clean suit and tie and got my spare felt hat off the top shelf in the closet.

Not wanting to take any more chances, I scooped my mail up in my hand, locked my front door behind me, and headed for the back stairway. Once outside I looked around for threats and finding none, hurried to my car. For the first five miles after leaving my apartment I kept my eye on my rearview mirror to see if I was being tailed. I was pretty sure I wasn't.

I stopped at another diner for lunch and read my mail as I ate. Most of it was bills and advertisement. I chucked the advertisements and stuffed the bills in my breast pocket. One letter was addressed to me in the neat hand I knew to be my girlfriend Billie's,. I opened it and read:

June 17, 1947

Dear Matt

This letter is hard to write. You are such a nice man, but you are too shy of commitment. I have met someone else. He's more in tune with my future hopes for a home and family. I'm sorry if this letter hurts you but this is for the best. I hope we can still be friends.
Yours truly
Billie.

The Brat: "How do you like that. While you're out saving damsels in distress and conspiring to slay the Bugsy dragon, this bitch sends you a 'Dear John' letter."

Captain Straight: "I didn't like her very much anyway."

The Brat: "Nobody did except for Little Matt, but you know how dumb he is."

My friends were only trying to make me feel better. Billie was my main squeeze and I knew I should be upset. But the funny thing was, the letter didn't bother me very much at all.

CHAPTER TWENTY

BEVERLY HILLS
JUNE 20, 1947
FRIDAY
7:55 P.M.

I parked my car a little way south of Virginia Hill's mansion, but across the street. I was close enough to have a good view of the front yard of 810 Linden Avenue, but far enough away that I didn't stick out like a sore thumb. About half of the available parking spaces on both sides of the street were occupied by parked cars, leaving plenty of spaces available. The sun's shadows were long and I knew it would be full dark within about thirty minutes. Even though any action wouldn't happen for at least a couple of hours, my heart was pulsing in my chest like a buzz bomb over the English Channel. I slid down in my seat, just high enough so that I could see out of the side window of my Hudson.

I rolled down my window and fired up a Camel cigarette. I inhaled a lungful of smoke and exhaled it. The smoke calmed me a little but not enough. I reached in my pocket and retrieved the pint bottle of Jack Daniel's bourbon I had bought at a liquor store an hour before and took a healthy pull on the neck.

The Brat: "When this little escapade is all over, are we going to reinstate the 'we only drink our bourbon from a glass' rule, or is it to go the way of the 'no bourbon until after six' rule we tried last month?"

Captain Straight: "For heaven's sake. Would you stop your babbling? Can't you see we're not in the mood for your poppycock?"

The Brat: "Have you any idea how stuffy and old man sounding you have gotten lately. The next thing you know you will be applying for a transfer to the head of a spinster schoolteacher. I can hear you now, 'Tell Billy not to slouch' and 'Johnny smells like he's been smoking.'"

Captain Straight: " In a couple of hours, Matt may be dodging a hail of bullets. This is no time for your bullshit."

"Guys," I said out loud, "If you two don't shut up right now when that hail of bullets comes, I'm going to stick my head out and yell 'hey' to the shooters. Maybe dodging a couple of .38 bullets whizzing through the Cerebral Cortex will teach you guys to tone it down, and finally put me out of my misery."

I had spent the afternoon in the cool balcony of a darkened movie theater. I chose this particular theater because of a sign out front that announced: "Cooled By Refrigeration." The movie playing was "Welcome Stranger" starring Bing Crosby, Joan Caulfield, and Barry Fitzgerald. I sat through three showings of the movie but slept through most of it. From what I saw during brief periods when I was awake, the movie was about a crusty old doctor, played by Fitzgerald, getting jealous when a young doctor, played by Bing, who was hired to replace him for a vacation, gets too popular with his patients.

I remembered that during one brief period when I was awake, the Brat was emphatically declaring that he didn't want any doctor while taking out HIS tonsils, "to be crooning "Mar zee Dotes and Do zee dotes," and not paying attention to business." This kind of thing was the reason I disliked going to the movies. I could never follow the storylines because The Brat would keep up a running commentary on the plot, the costumes, and the female star's bust size. Sometimes he even made up his own dialog. When I went to see a re-release of "Gone With The Wind" a while back, for weeks afterward he was imitating Vivian Leigh's southern accent and referring to Captain Straight as "Miss Scarlett," and Little Matt as "Mammy."

At 8:10 a cab pulled up in front of the mansion. Chick Hill got out accompanied by a pretty young woman and went inside. Chick was wearing a dark-colored suit and a black felt hat. Ten minutes later, a big black Cadillac emerged from behind the mansion, drove down the driveway and took off north toward Sunset Boulevard. I recalled what Tony had said in the Golden

Nugget Hotel about Siegel going out to dinner with Chick Hill, Chicks girlfriend and another guy tonight.

A little after 8:30, a big black Buick with four guys inside, drove slowly by the mansion without stopping. I recognized only one of the faces inside. It was that of the little squirrelly gangster who snatched me off the street and took me to Dragna's lawyer.

Captain Straight: "Why would Dragna's hoods be cruising by Siegel's house this late in the day?"

The Brat: "They're probably looking for the end of the line of guys waiting for a crack at Bugsy. It seems like half the population wants to kill Siegel. He really needs to take that Dale Carnegie course on winning friends and influencing people. Let's see now, Meyer Lansky and Lucky Luciano, according to Chick Hill, want to kill Siegel for skimming mob money. Chick Hill himself wants to kill Ben for beating up his sister. Dragna wants to kill him for knocking off his favorite nephew, and Tony wants to kill Siegel to protect Carmen. If I had that many guys after me, I'd just put my gun in my mouth and beat everyone to the punch."

Captain Straight: "Whoever the hell they are, they can't get a look at you. Matt, you need to scrunch down further in your seat."

The Brat: "Wouldn't it be a hoot if every faction that wants a crack at this gangster sends hit squads and they arrive and start shooting all at the same time? It'll be like the first twenty-minutes at Omaha Beach."

For the next two hours or so, I sat slumped in my Hudson as tense as a coiled spring. I was chain-smoking and tossing the butts out the window. During this time I also gave some thought to my escape route out of there. I decided I would high-tail it north on Linden to Sunset and then east to Beverly and turn south. After that, I would play it by ear.

Just after ten, the big black Cadillac came back, it turned left into Virginia's driveway, drove under the portico and disappeared behind the mansion. My body further stiffened with tension if that were possible. I took several deep breaths and another pull on my whiskey bottle to calm my nerves. The stage was set. The enemy had just entered the kill zone.

Nothing much happened for another half-hour. I saw the lights go on in the great room of the mansion. The drapes were pulled back on the big picture window facing the street. But I couldn't see much because the big pink lattice pagoda obscured most of my view of the interior.

I waited for a moment when no one was visible on the street and fired up the Hudson. I moved it closer to Virginia's mansion and parked across the street. From this angle, I had a much better view of the front of the mansion.

At 10:45 or so, I saw a guy walk out to the street from the south side of the house. He was wearing a dark suit and hat and strolling casually while puffing on a cigarette. I couldn't make out his facial features but I was pretty sure the guy was Chick Hill. This man walked like Hill walked and had on a dark suit similar to the one Chick was wearing when he got out of the cab a couple of hours ago. The man stood on the sidewalk, still smoking, and carefully looked both directions up and down the street.

I cringed back in my car. The last thing I needed was for Chick Hill to spot me in a car outside the house where Bugsy Siegel was staying. If Tony did kill Bugsy in the next hour, Hill would be able to tell the cops later that I was sitting in front of the place the whole time the shooting was going on.

But the guy didn't spot me and come over to chat. Instead, he flipped his cigarette butt into the street, turned and began walking not back the way he had come, but toward the pink pagoda in the front yard. That seemed weird to me. Why was he going over there? When he got to the pagoda, the man in the dark suit crouched down and retrieved a long object from under the lattice structure. At first, I couldn't tell what the object was, but when the man brought it to his shoulder and pointed it toward the picture window on the front of the house, I knew what it was. It was some kind of rifle, but it was so dark I couldn't discern details of the weapon.

What happened next has been permanently burned into my memory. It has played out in my mind thousands of times since then, like film clip from a newsreel.

Nine shots boomed out in rapid succession. I saw flames leap from the barrel of the rifle with each shot and the noise was deafening on the quiet street. When he finished shooting, the guy in the dark suit almost casually flung the rifle by its barrel onto the pavement of the street. I saw the weapon skid across the blacktop and come to rest next to the car parked directly in front of mine. The shooter then ducked back along the south side of the mansion and out of my sight.

I immediately turned the ignition key and hit the starter button on my Hudson. I had to get out of there right away. The engine roared to life and I popped the clutch and the car leaped forward. As I came even with where the rifle was laying in the street, I did a strange thing. I stopped my car momentarily, opened the door and picked up the gunman's discarded rifle. Tossing the weapon on my passenger seat, I slammed the door, gunned my motor and got the hell out of there.

The Brat: "What the hell did you do that for? You do realize that if the cops catch you with that rifle in your car they will think that you're the shooter."

In the back of my mind, I was asking myself the same question. Almost immediately I knew the answer. Since I thought the shooter was Chick Hill, I was just trying to keep a fellow

Marine veteran and a good guy out of trouble. Still, it was an absolutely crazy thing to do.

Once I was a few blocks away, on Sunset Boulevard, I slowed down to twenty-five miles per hour. Two Beverly Hills police cars with red lights flashing and sirens wailing flashed by me going the opposite way. In my rearview mirror, I watched them turn left on Linden Drive. I turned right on Beverly and escaped into the night.

When I got to my apartment, I didn't worry about whether there were gangsters there waiting to kill me. I was too emotionally and physically drained. Either Bugsy Siegel was alive or he was dead. If he was dead then I was home free. If he was alive, then it was probably only a matter of time before I was dead instead of him. I was so spent that I didn't care much, either way. I figured I was in the clear regarding the shooting. If any of the neighbors happened to get the license number of the Hudson, it couldn't be traced back to me. I had bought the car for cash and didn't show identification to the car salesman. After bringing the assassin's rifle up to my apartment wrapped in my suit jacket and putting it in my bedroom closet, I fell on the bed and slept the dreamless sleep of the totally exhausted.

§

When I awoke I was groggy and my mouth tasted like the Black Hole of Calcutta must have smelled. Thirty cigarettes and almost a pint of bourbon the previous night will do that to you every time. Looking at my watch. I saw it was 7:43 A.M. I got up, stripped, and left my clothes where they fell on the floor. While the bathtub was filling, I brushed my teeth and shaved. After getting out of the tub, I dressed in clean linen and a fresh shirt and put on the suit I wore the previous day.

The Brat: "How much longer are you going to keep us in suspense. We have to go get a newspaper and find out what the hell happened last night."

He was right. I retrieved my hat from the pile of clothes on the floor, went downstairs and across the street to a newsstand where I bought the morning editions of the Times and the Herald Examiner. I took the papers back to my apartment and spread then out on my kitchen table.

The Herald-Examiner had the more lurid details. Across the top of the front page was a banner headline: "BUGSY SIEGEL SLAIN." Underneath there was a picture of the dead mobster sprawled half in and half out of a chair, with a bloody face and chest. The article underneath the picture said that Siegel was killed by shots fired through the picture window of his girlfriend's mansion from outside. Bugsy was hit by four bullets, two in the chest and two on the right side of his face. One of the shots to his face had dislodged his left eye, that was found across the room. Alan Smiley, a friend, and business associate of Siegel's, was in the room when the shots rang out and sustained minor injuries.

I gathered up the papers and dumped them in the kitchen trash can. So it was over. Carmen and I were safe. There was absolutely no reason for anyone to come after us. The best part was that I wouldn't have the participation in a murder on my conscience. Tony, Carlo and I had planned to kill Bugsy, but Chick Hill had beaten us to it. At least I thought the killer was Chick. Because it was dark I couldn't be one hundred percent sure.

I locked my apartment, went downstairs and got in my Hudson. The first order of business was breakfast. I went to Nick's Café on Spring Street. While eating my pancakes I reflected on all the crazy shit that had happened to me since I was last there.

Next, I went to the garage where I stored my Oldsmobile. It was covered by about an inch of dirt. I paid an attendant to wash it for me and while I waited told the owner that I would like to store the Hudson there. He agreed and I gave him a ten-dollar deposit against the storage fees. In about three months, the owner of the garage would go to civil court and obtain permission to sell the car to pay the owing storage fees. I sincerely hoped that a worthy person would end up with it. It was a fine old automobile and had served me well. When my Oldsmobile was ready, I transferred my two dirty suits from the trunk of the Hudson and drove out of the lot.

It felt strange to park my car in my designated space in front of my office. It almost seemed as if the escapades of the past two weeks had been just a bad dream brought on by too much booze, nicotine, and adrenaline. I got out and rode the elevator to my floor like I had done hundreds of times before. The office looked the same. The people looked the same, except for Betty. She had a concerned look on her face.

"Oh Mr. Cole, I've been frantic for three days. You have to call a woman named Florence Carter at this number," she said and handed me a slip of paper with a phone number written on it. "Your father is gravely ill."

CHAPTER TWENTY ONE

LOS ANGELES
JUNE 21, 1947
SATURDAY
10:30 A.M.

I rushed to my office and dialed the long-distance operator. It took over two minutes for the call to be put through. Finally, I heard the phone on the other end begin to ring.

"Hello, this is Flo Carter."

"Hi, My name is Matthew Cole, I was given this num…"

"Oh Matthew, thank God you have finally called. I'm Florence Carter. Your father and I have been together for many years."

"Yes, My father told me all about you. It's a pleasure to finally speak to you. What is wrong with my dad."

"He caught a cold on the train returning from his visit with you. I tried to get him to go to the doctor but he wouldn't go as usual. Now, his doctor has told me that the infection has turned into pneumonia. He's gravely ill and sinking fast. He wants to speak to you one last time. Can you get here as soon as you can?"

"I'm on my way. Tell him I love him."

"He knows that."

My brain was in such a muddle that I didn't know what to do first. I stumbled out of my office into the area behind the reception desk. Mrs. Adderley came out of her office, saw me and came over to me frowning.

"Mr. Cole, are you ill? You're white as a sheet."

"I think my father's dying in Seattle. I have to get there quickly but my brain isn't working right."

"LUANN," shouted Mrs. Adderley. The aide flew around a corner into our sight and skidded to a stop breathlessly.

"Luann, Get on the phone to the airlines. Book the most direct and shortest duration flight to Seattle, Washington for Mr.

Cole. Tell them time is of the essence. Call me at Mr. Coles apartment with the flight information."

"Yes, Ma'am," answered Luann and ran off.

"Come with me. I'll drive you. We'll swing by your apartment and pack a bag of essentials on our way to the airport," said Mrs. Adderley, taking charge. We went downstairs to her car and headed toward my apartment. Mrs. Adderley was an aggressive driver, going over the speed limit and weaving in and out of traffic, which surprised me. Most women drove cautiously.

When we walked into my apartment Mrs. Adderley put her hands on her hips and stared at the disarray. "I think you should either hire a housekeeper or two strong men to shovel this place out once a month so you can start over," she said as she sniffed the air. I didn't reply, but The Brat did.

The Brat: "Watch out. Before you know it she'll have Betty and Luann in here cleaning up, but Betty will be doing all the work while Luann flies around the room like a Japanese Zero."

"Sit down, and don't do anything," said Mrs. Adderley "Where is the bedroom?" I pointed her in the right direction and she bustled off to pack my things.

The Brat: "I bet by the time we get back from Seattle, this apartment will have been converted into a combination storage room and guest quarters for rich clients."

With perfect timing, as usual, Mrs. Adderley walked out of the bedroom carrying my smallest suitcase and the phone rang. "I'll get that. It will be Luann for me," she said. She picked up the phone receiver, exchanged short clipped sentences with Luann and then put the receiver back on its cradle.

"You're booked on Western Airlines flight 341, out of Los Angeles Municipal Airport.   It's a non-stop flight to San Francisco. You will have a thirty-minute layover there and then board Western flight 254, non-stop to Seattle. Your flight leaves Los Angeles in one hour and twenty minutes. I suggest we leave now and get you checked in early, before the last-minute rush."

"Thank you, Mrs. Adderley. You are very efficient," I replied.

"Of course I am, that's my job," she said with a dismissive look.

§

I checked in at the airline counter where they took my small suitcase. We were directed to gate three. It was easy enough to find, we just followed the signs with arrows. The departure gate waiting area was outside on the tarmac, under an awning. We stood just inside the door of the terminal because it was a very warm day.

"Your flight boards in twenty minutes," said Mrs. Adderley. "I will stay with you until you're on the plane just in case there is something else you think needs to be done in your absence. Here are your tickets. You will have to make your own arrangements for the return flight since your return date is unknown. I will call ahead and inform the person you are to meet in Seattle of your flight number."

"How do you know who it is? I seem to have lost the message slip that Betty gave me."

"I'll get it off the phone log. Another of my new innovations" replied Mrs. Adderley.

"Mrs. Adderley, why are you doing all this. I would think that with the way I rag on you all the time you wouldn't like me very much," I said.

"Do you think I dislike you?"

"I don't know, but I would if I was in your place."

"Oh, you stupid, stupid man. Let me tell you a few things. When I was growing up I wasn't like the other little girls. I didn't play with dolls or play house. I was and still, am fascinated with the business world. When I grew older, I decided I didn't want to get married and have children. I wanted to someday run a big company. I went to business college to prepare myself. When I entered the business world, I was in for a rude awakening.

Because I was a woman, my ideas weren't respected. During meetings, I was the one ordered to make coffee and serve it to the men at the conference table. I toiled for years in a business career that was a frustrating disaster. No one would give me a chance to prove myself."

"Then one day I answered an ad for an office manager at your agency. Your business was a disorganized mess and I set about making it better and more profitable. I instituted policies that you questioned, but you never interfered with me and never countermanded my orders. You just made some bad jokes and drank your whiskey, but you gave me my chance. Well, Mr. Cole, I have proven myself. I turned a detective agency on its last legs into the third largest and most profitable one in Los Angeles. And I plan for it to be number one in the near future. Dislike you, Mr. Cole? No, I don't dislike you. I'm very grateful to you."

"But that doesn't mean I don't think you are the most exasperating human being I have ever met and have forgiven you for turning those preachers loose on me. And don't think that I won't fight you tooth and nail in the future about the management of the agency."

"Mrs. Adderley, Caroline, I don't know what to say."

"Don't say anything, just get on the damn plane."

§

The airplane I boarded was a Douglas DC-3 painted in the colors of Western Airlines. The same plane, known as the C-47 by the Army, the R4D by the Navy and Marines, "Dakota" by the British, and "Goony bird" by most American servicemen, was the workhorse for the Allied air transport commands during the late war. It had been shown to be a marvelous airplane able to take considerable punishment and still keep flying. I had read in the Los Angeles times that the airlines were in the process of retiring all the DC-3s in favor of the new four-engined Douglas DC-6, and the Lockheed Constellation. But on this route, Western Airlines still flew the venerable DC-3.

There were thirty-four seats for passengers on the DC-3. About a quarter of the seats were empty as I limped down the center aisle from the entry door. Each row had two seats on each side of the aisle. All the people already seated were dressed to the nines. Flying was still enough of a novelty that people dressed in their Sunday best before getting on an airliner. I chose an aisle seat on the right that I judged was over the center of the wing and sat down.

In the window seat next to me was an overweight, florid faced man in a dark suit and multi-colored tie. He was smoking a cigarette and reading a newspaper.

And then I saw her. The woman who was to figure so prominently in my future came walking down the aisle telling the passengers to fasten their seat belts. She was tall for a woman, slim, with a prominent bust and long shapely legs. Her blonde hair was worn pinned up under a little blue hat that looked like a modified military barracks cap, with a stylized wing pinned to the front on the left side. She was wearing a blue stewardess uniform, resembling a woman's business suit, with a full set of wings above the swell of her breasts on the left side. Her face was oval with a long, straight nose and two large, wide-set, friendly blue eyes, and her generous lips were smiling pleasantly. Little Matt came awake like Dracula at the stroke of midnight.

Little Matt: "Oh wow! Now that's' the kind of woman I go for. Why don't you ever get me somebody like her?"

The Brat: "Steady there stupid, wait till you hear her speak. She might be the mental twin of Carmen Cardello."

The pilot picked that minute to come on the intercom: "Good afternoon ladies and gentlemen, this is your pilot, Captain Peterson. On behalf of second officer Connors and cabin stewardess, Miss Chalmers, I'd like to welcome you aboard Western Airlines flight 341 to San Francisco. We should be on the ground in San Francisco in about two hours and forty minutes. Flying conditions are excellent, so, sit back, relax and enjoy the flight."

The Brat: "The bastard might be lying. I don't trust voices where I can't see the person speaking."

Captain Straight: "You can't really see me, and we talk all the time."

The brat: "That's right. I don't trust voices where I can't see the person speaking. That's why I've never trusted you either."

Captain straight: "Well, so far, so good. It looks like we'll probably have a smooth flight, not a cloud in the sky."

The Brat: "Yeah, it looks great. Of course, that asshole upfront at the controls may have been up all night swilling booze and partying with three nubile stewardesses, and is still so drunk he thinks he is in Cleveland. Yeah, everything is peachy."

The Brat was afraid to fly. He denied being scared and said he just didn't like it. But every time we flew and the pilot gunned his engines and started his takeoff roll, The Brat was scared shitless. This flight was no exception.

The pilot applied power to his two idling engines and the airplane surged forward and rumbled slowly on the taxiway toward the threshold of the runway. The DC-3 then slewed around, the pilot aligning the aircraft with the runway, and then the two big engines suddenly rose to maximum power and we were off. The aircraft gradually gathered speed as it traveled down the runway.

The Brat: "What if that drunken idiot up front has a heart attack just as we're leaving the ground?"

As the lift generated over the wings took effect, I felt the rear of the airliner rise. The cabin floor was no longer slanted but level.

The Brat: "It's taking too long! We're not going to make it. I was right all along, these contraptions are deathtraps."

Suddenly the rumbling noise and vibration stopped and the ride became smooth as glass. We were in the air. The "Gooneybird" was suddenly in its element, where it was designed to be.

Captain Straight: "You okay buddy?"

The Brat: "Shut up and suggest that Matt order a drink. I could use one."

A while back I investigated a wealthy businessman suspected of cheating om his wife. He spent weekends with his spouse at their Beverly Hills mansion, then flew to Sacramento on Monday and stayed there all week. Following him entailed flying with the man to and from Sacramento. Before I finally caught the fat cat with his mistress, I made about ten flights with him. On every flight, The Brat acted the exact same way as he had just acted. I knew he would freak out again when it came the time to land. And Lord help us if we ran into any turbulence.

CHAPTER TWENTY-TWO

ELEVEN THOUSAND FEET OVER SANTA BARBARA
JUNE 21, 1947
SATURDAY
1: OO P.M.

About twenty minutes into the flight, The gorgeous Miss Chalmers came by and took drink orders for my seatmate and I. The florid faced businessman ordered a scotch and soda. I ordered, what else? Bourbon on the rocks. While waiting for our drinks to be served my seatmate introduced himself.

"Hello, I'm Jim Danton. I'm a regional sales manager for Smallwood Industries. We sell Forklift trucks."

"Matt Cole. I run a detective agency.'

"Detective Huh? I once had one a you guys after me. My ex-wife hired him. No hard feelings though," said Danton as he lit up a cigarette.

Miss Chalmers came with our drinks on a little tray. As she was serving them, Danton, folded a section of his newspaper and shoved it under my nose. The article his stubby finger pointed to was headlined: "ANOTHER JEWISH IMMIGRANT SHIP ATTEMPTS TO RUN BRITISH BLOCKADE OF PALESTINE."

"I feel sorry for the British," said Danton while taking a drag on his cigarette. "But better them than us. We got enough Jews in America."

The Brat: "Way to go slick, You had to pick a seat next to an anti-Semitic bigot. Next, he'll be telling you how the Jews run the government."

"We got a real Jew problem in our own government. All those Republicans in Congress are Jew lovers and are bein' paid off by the Hebes. If it wasn't for the Democrats from the South holdin' the line, the Jews would control everything." As my seatmate was speaking, I looked up into the face of the lovely Miss Chalmers. I saw revulsion and distaste in her glance at Danton.

The Brat: "Just let this asshole have a peek at your gun and tell him your name is really Cohen. That'll shut the bastard up."

I was tempted to do what The Brat said, but not wanting to create a scene on the airplane, I folded my arms, turned away from Danton and ignored him. A few minutes later Miss Chalmers was back. She leaned down so she could be heard above the engine noise.

"Excuse me sir, but the Captain has informed me that we have a little problem with weight distribution that's making it hard for him to properly trim the airplane. I'm afraid you will have to follow me to another seat."

I picked up my drink and followed the beautiful stewardess to the rear of the plane. She showed me to an aisle seat in the last row that was directly across from two seats labeled, "Flight crew only." Before she walked away to resume her duties, I leaned close and whispered, "Thanks for rescuing me." She just smiled at me in return.

About an hour and forty minutes into the flight Miss Chalmers returned to the rear of the plane and sat down in the seat across from me. We began to talk. At first, our conversation was light-hearted banter. Then I found myself telling her about my life. She listened without interruption which is a rare gift. Most people want to jump in and interrupt the narrative to talk about themselves. I got the feeling she was really listening, not just being polite. I told her about my off-again, on-again relationship with my father and growing up in Los Angeles. I told her about my going off to war and returning nearly crippled. She, however, offered very little information about herself in return.

About forty minutes before we were to land she excused herself saying she had to prepare for landing. I didn't want to see her go.

"Is there any chance that you would have dinner with me some evening?" I asked.

She looked genuinely sad when she replied: "I'm sorry but we're not allowed to date passengers. I could lose my job."

"At least tell me your name," I said.

"It's June, June Chalmers," she said with a smile that made Little Matt do several backflips.

The landing was routine, but to The Brat, it was a harrowing experience. As the pilot put the plane in a glide toward the runway, he couldn't help himself.

The Brat: "We're coming in too steep. Somebody needs to tell that drunken fool to get the stewardess off his lap and pay attention."

I was at the end of the pack in the deplaning crowd. As I walked down the metal stairway I saw that the terminal was a Quonset hut. The day was cloudy and damp. I could see puddles of water on the asphalt around me. apparently, it had just rained. I walked toward this Quonset hut and saw a tall woman standing behind a chain-link fence. She was holding an umbrella in one hand and a handwritten sign with my name on it in the other. As

I got closer to her I saw that she was in her fifties with grey hair worn down on her shoulders. Her clothing wasn't flashy, just a simple flowered, and belted dress covered by a green sweater, but the way she carried herself spoke of class. I felt that she could dress in a flour sack and she would still look striking. I passed through the gate and approached the woman. She dropped the sign, came up to me and put a hand on each side of my shoulders. Her voice was deep and soothing.

"Are you Matthew Cole?"

"Yeah, that's me," I replied.

"I'm Florence Carter. Your father and I have been together for many years. I hate to be the one to tell you this, but your father passed away this afternoon. I am so sorry."

I was in shock. Florence had to lead me by the hand to her car. It was a late model maroon Cadillac convertible. During the drive to my now late father's house, I didn't speak. I was too busy berating myself.

Why did I spend so much time on a case involving Bugsy Siegel, Tony Cardello, and other trash, instead of coming to Seattle with my dad? If I had chucked everything and come, I would have had another week or so with him before he died. The Brat was also pounding on me.

244 | D.W. DRAKE

The Brat: "Why are you always ignoring the important things in life to focus on bullshit that means nothing. It turns out that you're a shitty son after all."

I don't know how long the drive was, I was all wrapped up in my grief and self-loathing, But eventually, we turned into a driveway that wound through landscaped grounds and stopped in front of a house that appeared to be entirely constructed of redwood stained dark red. It wasn't especially big, but the hill it sat on had a magnificent view of a lake or ocean inlet, I couldn't tell which.

"I'll show you to your room," said Florence. "I'm sure you want to be alone for a while."

§

I spent a hellish night grieving and beating up on myself. It involved about a quart of bourbon and a pack or two of cigarettes. Just after midnight, I lost consciousness, but I was more passed out drunk than asleep. I awoke early the next morning with a gargantuan hangover. The sadistic little men with jackhammers chipping away at the interior of my skull were extra enthusiastic that morning. My tongue was furry and foul-tasting and I bet my breath would remove paint from any metal surface. I searched through my suitcase for aspirin, but there wasn't any there.

The Brat: "Mrs. Adderley should have known about your frequent hangovers and included aspirin in your suitcase. You should remind her when you see her that she fell down on her job."

I decided I needed two things on an emergency basis, coffee, and aspirin. I didn't want to roam the halls of a strange house looking like a wino from skid row so I cleaned up first. I shaved, combed my hair and put on clean boxers and shirt as well as the suit I wore the day before. It was the only one I brought with me. When I was done my image looked more or less presentable in the mirror mounted over the dresser in my room.

I stepped into the hall outside my room and went down the stairs holding onto the handrail. The delicious aroma of frying bacon led me to a large kitchen. A well-fed, apple-cheeked, smiling woman wearing an apron was there leaning over a stove. She saw me and her smile widened.

"You must be Matthew Cole, Flo told me you would be joining us. I'm Minnie. I'm the housekeeper, cook, sometimes maid and soon to be a gardener if that lazy man we hired doesn't get off his rear end and do something about the weeds down by the sound. How can I serve you sir?" she said. Her smile was infectious and I found myself returning it despite my hangover.

"I need aspirin, coffee and maybe some of that bacon," I replied.

"Just have a seat at the table there and give me a few minutes and I'll fix you right up," said the cook.

I sat as directed. She brought the coffee and aspirin first and said the breakfast would take a few minutes more. I smiled and nodded in acknowledgment. As I was taking my first grateful sip of coffee the kitchen door opened and a tall, athletic-looking man in his late thirties entered. He was dressed in white tennis shorts, a white shirt and had a blue sweater draped over his shoulders with the arms hanging down in front. In his hands was a tennis racket. The guy had a smug, smirk on his handsome face.

"You must be Bob's prodigal son," said the man.

"Yes, I'm Robert Cole's son. Who are you?" I asked.

"I'm Quentin Carter, Flo's brother."

"Nice to meet you," I replied. He didn't come over to shake my hand and I didn't rise and go to him either. I detected an undercurrent of hostility in the tone of his speech.

"When an animal on the Serengeti Plain falls ill and is about to die, the carrion birds fly in from all over to be in on the kill," said Quentin with a sneer.

"Now Quentin, you shouldn't talk like that," said Minnie the cook.

"Shut up and cook. This is none of your business Minnie. You need

to remember your place here. You're a servant.," Quentin hissed.

"Look asshole," I said, getting angry, "My dad died yesterday and I'm not in the mood to put up with rude pricks at the moment. So you'd better get out of here or I'll walk you down to that lake, inlet or sound, or whatever the fuck you call it and throw you in it."

"How dare you speak to me like that. You're not satisfied to come here to rob my sister of her rightful inheritance, but you call me rude names and threaten me in the bargain."

"What are you talking about?" I asked.

"My sister Florence wasted the best years of her life living with your father. Then when he dies, he leaves most of his money to a supposed son who he hadn't seen in years. Do you think you can just waltz in here and leave with two million dollars? Well. Think again."

"Quintin, shut up and leave this house, and don't come back until you can act like a decent human being," said Florence angrily. Neither Quintin or I had noticed her walk into the kitchen.

'But Flo, I was just trying to protect your interests," protested Quintin.

"Oh, I doubt that. I think you need the money and you're here to try to get some from Robert's estate. Why else would you be here? You and Robert didn't get along. I was listening in the hall and I heard you talking about carrion birds. Well, Quintin, the only buzzard I see here at the moment is you."

"Alright, I'll leave," said a red-faced and furious Quintin, "but this isn't over and I won't forget this." He pointed his finger at me, " watch out," he said and then disappeared out the kitchen door.

Florence turned to me with embarrassment on her face. " Will you accept my apology for my brother?"

"No problem. We can pick our friends but not our family," I replied.

"Do you mind if I join you for breakfast?" she asked.

"Not at all, it would be my pleasure."

"I feel you're due a further explanation for my brother's behavior," said Florence as she sat down across from me. "Both my brother and I came from a wealthy family and are trust fund babies. I received my share of the inheritance from my father in a lump sum. Quentin, on the other hand, received his in seven equal installments spaced ten years apart. My father did it this way because my brother is such a wastrel, that he would have spent his whole inheritance the first six months if he got it all at once. I imagine that he's running low on funds and his next installment isn't due until he turns forty, in three years' time. When my brother starts to worry about maintaining his lifestyle, he gets nastier than usual."

"You don't have to explain anything to me," I replied. "I fact, if you need some of the money my dad left to me to live on, I'll gladly let you have it."

"That won't be necessary. Your father left me this house and sufficient funds that, combined with my own money, will allow me to live out my life here in comfort. Thanks for offering though."

Our conversation drifted away from money as Minnie the cook served us platters laden with fried eggs, bacon and waffles. The sugar in the food, as well as the aspirin, revived me and my hangover went away. As we got more comfortable with each other, the topics of our conversation became lighter. I asked Florence how she and my father had met. She replied that she was on vacation to Seattle with some of her college classmates. She went to a party and met my father. They were immediately attracted to each other. They ended up leaving the party and walking on the beach until dawn. She had thought that that would be the end of it and she would go back to New York and remember the time with my dad as just a pleasant interlude. But she couldn't get him out of her mind. Florence returned to Seattle and they moved in together. Marriage was out of the question because my mother refused to give my father a divorce.

"So we lived together. I left him a bunch of times in the early years but found myself so miserable without him that I came back and finally stayed. But if I had told any of my girlfriends at college that I was going to shack up for twenty-years with a guy who made mustard, they would have had me locked up in the loony bin," said Florence laughing.

§

The funeral was the typical barbaric ritual it was designed to be and confirmed the soundness of my long-standing policy of avoiding them if at all possible. There was something weird and distasteful for a group of people to gather with the dead guy laid out in front of them, nose pointed at the ceiling while a minister spouts insincere platitudes for a half hour. Alone among civilized western societies, the Irish are the only ones who do it right. They put the deceased in the ground pronto, and then they go and get drunk in the dead guy's honor. In any case, I got through the funeral more or less intact and didn't break down in tears or anything.

That evening after the last glass of chardonnay was drunk, the last pig in a blanket eaten and the last mourner went home, Florence, Her asshole brother Quentin and I sat ourselves down in my father's study for the reading of my father's will. Sitting behind the big mahogany desk was a guy who identified himself as Milton Krebs, my dad's attorney.

After boiling off the whereases and wheretos and other legalese, the document was pretty straightforward. Florence would receive the house, a ski cabin in Sun Valley, cars, and a sum of money privately agreed upon by Flo and my father, that would be sufficient for her to maintain her current lifestyle until her death. I was to receive all remaining assets of the estate, in the amount of two million, one hundred and forty-seven thousand dollars. When the lawyer read off the amount I looked over at Quentin. He was glaring at me with hate in his eyes.

"I protest this miscarriage of justice. My sister is getting screwed by this outrage," said Quentin.

"You can protest all you want," said the lawyer, Milton Krebs, " but this will is legally ironclad. I invite you to try to contest it. You'll only waste your money. Besides, you have no standing to protest anything."

As we got up to leave Mr. Krebs handed me an envelope. It was addressed simply to "Matt."

I put it in my breast pocket and headed toward the door. On the way, I was intercepted by Quentin Carter. "I need to speak to you for a moment," he said, led me to an empty room near the pantry and closed the door for privacy.

"I'll make a deal with you. Give me half of what the old man gave you and I won't make trouble for you," said Quintin. I didn't answer, I just stared at him. " I know plenty of people who can make your life miserable. People of our class stick together and know how to put nobody's like you in their place," he continued.

"Well Quintin old buddy, Your sister told me that you needed money, but I didn't know how badly you needed it until now. If you had come to me and asked nicely, I might have shared some of the money with you. But with you threatening me, I have decided to not give you shit. In fact, if you don't leave right now, I'm going to kick your ass from here to Portland."

"Don't think that this is over," Quintin said through gritted teeth. "You'll find out what happens when you mess with the Carter family."

That evening as I was packing for my departure the next day, I came across the envelope that the lawyer had given me. I opened the letter and read:

June 20, 1947

Dear Matt

I'm sorry this note is typewritten and not in my own hand. It's hard to write with oxygen masks and all the other tubes attached to my body. I so wanted to see you one last time, but it looks like it is not to be. I want to say that I'm proud to call you my son. I grieve for all the things we missed in our long separation. I have left you a considerable sum of money and I'm sure you will be intimidated by its size and will be wondering where to put it so it's safe. I have taken the liberty to have my lawyer, Milt Krebs invest the money in an appropriate portfolio for you. You can trust Milt, he's honest and a straight shooter. You can accept his advice or ignore him, that's up to you, but just remember, it's only money and thus is not very important in the long run. Don't let it rule your life.

I ask you to keep a discrete eye on Flo and protect her if you can. She has some members of her family that are absolute snakes. She would kill me early if she knew I was writing this, so never let on that I encouraged you to keep in touch.

Well, that's all your old man has to say. I don't' exactly know what awaits me on the other side but as for this life, I feel that having you as my son was the main reason I was put on this earth. Goodbye son.

Your loving father
Robert Matthew Cole.

CHAPTER TWENTY-THREE

HUNTINGTON BEACH
JULY 16, 1947
WEDNESDAY
11:00 A.M.

F amily sedans, stylish coupes, and jalopies, no doubt it was high school kids that owned the jalopies, lined both sides of US 101 as I drove south, passing the Huntington Beach pier.   The spectacular summer day had brought an overflow crowd to the beaches on each side of the pier even though it was a weekday. The ocean here was known for its clear green-tinted water, almost entirely devoid of sea kelp.

I ran over a section of washed-out pavement on Route 101 but I barely felt it. The suspension of my new, Pinehurst Green, 1947 Cadillac five-passenger touring sedan easily negotiated any section of rough road. I sat on white leather seats with my left arm on the sill of the window and my right gripping the genuine walnut steering wheel. I was wearing one of my new custom-tailored suits. This one a muted dove gray wool. The fabric in the suit was so smooth that when you ran your hand over it, you swore it was cut from angel's wings.

The car and the suits were my only concessions so far to my newfound wealth. I probably would rent a bigger apartment when I got around to it, and hire a day maid, but other than that, I couldn't think of anything else I wanted. I didn't want to stop being a detective. I wanted everything to go on as before.

I took the train home from Seattle instead of an airplane. The Brat had badgered me endlessly on the morning of my departure date, saying things like: "We're in no hurry this time. Why risk life and limb flying in one of those deathtraps? On the train, we can just take our time and stay firmly rooted to the ground." I finally relented and took the train.

Before going to the train station, I had Flo stop at a newsstand where I bought as many back copies of the Los Angeles Times and other L.A. papers that the newsboy could find in the backroom of his kiosk. The leisurely trip south gave me an opportunity to read all the articles that had been written in the Times regarding the Bugsy Siegel killing. Gory detail followed gory detail and wild speculation abounded. Most of the public assumed that the murder was a gangland hit. The New York mob did little to quell this public opinion. After all, they couldn't let a perfectly good bloody gangland killing go to waste, could they? Bugsy was skimming money from the Flamingo Hotel and the New York mob killed him for it was the rumor that they intentionally spread. Jack Dragna got his revenge, another "expert" on the underworld told a reporter. One source even said that it was a mob hit paid for by Virginia Hill. In any event, the police investigation so far had come up empty. They had no suspects and no murder weapon. I chuckled when I read that. The murder weapon was stashed in my closet in Los Angeles.

A few days after I returned to Los Angeles, Milton Krebs came to see me at my office. He sat across from me and detailed the investments he had made with my inherited money.

"I have put one million each into blue-chip stocks and tax-free government bonds. I would suggest that you leave this money alone and allow it to work for you. The remaining money I divided between a savings account at Bank of America in the amount of $100,000 and a checking account in the amount of $47,000. Please sign these signature cards, so I can return them to the bank, your checks should arrive in the mail within about two weeks." said Krebs and pushed two cards across the desk.

"Anytime you want to alter this arrangement, just contact me in Seattle and I will take a train down here. I really liked your dad and I want to assist you in any way I can," said Krebs.

"Am I in any legal jeopardy from Quintin, Flo's brother regarding the inheritance?"

"I wouldn't worry about that. The will has been structured in such a way as to preclude any shenanigans from that quarter."

After the lawyer left I told Mrs. Adderley that I was calling a mandatory meeting of all my employees for that afternoon at four. I told her that I had something important to tell all the employees. Everyone was on pins and needles wondering what I was going to say. Mrs. Adderley tried to pump me for information just after lunch but I remained mum. I could tell she thought that I was going to close the business, I could see the glum disappointment on her face.

At four I stood up on a chair in the reception area to address my employees. The young detectives were gathered at the rear and the typists, and other miscellaneous employees were at the front. Betty and Luann were already close to tears, fearing the worst.

"I've never called one of these meetings before," I started off, " but I felt I just had to do it this time. I've got a real problem with your work product lately," I said with a somber face and paused.

I saw the anger on the faces of most of the workers. Some of the females were crying. Mrs. Adderley wore a shocked expression.

"So I'll just have to do something to motivate you. How about this? At the end of the year, I'll take fifty percent of the net company profits and give them to all of you as a Christmas bonus. Everybody gets an equal share, from office manager to the guy who sweeps up at night," I said and grinned.

There was silence for about the space of three heartbeats as my employees absorbed my words. Then pandemonium broke out. The next day, Mrs. Adderley came into my office and sat down.

"I know what you did yesterday was out of kindness, and because of your new-found wealth. But those people out there are so motivated that I think most of them would try to run through a brick wall if you asked them to do it. I can't be sure yet, but I figure that with the heightened productivity of your employees, you will probably make nearly as much money this year, as you would if you hadn't made your kind gesture."

The next day I had Mrs. Adderley prepare an invoice in the amount of $500 for services rendered. I sent it to Tony Cardello, care of the Flamingo Hotel in Las Vegas. I hadn't heard back from him since. I suppose I could go there and see Tony to demand payment, and he might even pay me if I showed up there. But I also might end up sharing the bottom of that mine shaft with Vinnie. I decided I wouldn't press the matter. In fact, I sincerely hoped that I never saw tony Cardello and Carlo the mountain and a half ever again.

About a week and a half after I got back from Seattle, a gossip columnist for the Herald examiner complicated my life. The writer told about a local young private eye named Matt Cole who had just inherited over two million dollars. Everywhere I went now, I seemed to be running into smiling babes. Little Matt had been like a kid in a candy store lately.

I also began to receive letters and phone messages from my ex-girlfriend, Billie. I wouldn't take the calls, but in her letters, she said she had been mistaken in breaking up with me and professed her undying love. She even subtly intimated in one of her perfumed missives that her little rule about sex before marriage might not be so hard and fast. I guess I could have contacted her and listened to her pitch, but I realized that I didn't care about her that much, even with the prospect of finally getting her into bed.

I stopped for lunch at a beachside cafe in a rundown little town clinging to the cliffs above the ocean. It was an artist's colony called Laguna beach. Afterward, I continued my drive along the water. The views were spectacular. At irregular intervals, I passed through little beach towns like Dana Point and San Clemente. When I entered the town of Oceanside, I saw a sign, turned left and stopped at a white-painted, stucco guard post. A big sign announced the post as: "Marine Base Camp Pendleton."

I told the sentry that I needed to go where the 3rd Marine Brigade was quartered. After checking my identification, the sentry gave me a little mimeographed map and sent me off to follow it to my destination. I found out pretty quick just how huge Camp Pendleton was. It took me over an hour on dirt roads to locate the headquarters of the 3rd Marine Brigade. The duty sergeant told me to wait in a nearby recreation room while he located Corporal Charles Hill.

Chick acted like he was glad to see me when he walked in about thirty minutes later. He had on green dungarees, stained by dark patches of sweat. He strode over to a coke machine, put two nickels in and got two bottles. He handed me a bottle and took a sip from the neck of the other.

"Matt Cole, what the hell are you doing here?"

"I came to return your M1 carbine. You know, the one you used to kill Bugsy Siegel."

He reacted the way I thought he would. His eyes grew cold and calculating and the smile slipped from his face. " Whoa, there friend," he replied, "who says I killed Ben Siegel?"

"I do. I was sitting across the street in a parked car and saw you do it. Was that carbine your duty weapon?"

"Do you think I am that stupid to use my duty weapon to commit a murder? I think you're nuts. This whole conversation is nuts."

"Oh, I'm not condemning you. Far from it. At the time you killed that bastard he had his boys out trying to kill me, so, actually I am kinda indebted to you." I said.

"I still say you got the wrong guy. But just as a hypothetical, what if some guy gets tired of another guy beating up on his sister. He finally has enough so he goes to a pawnshop in San Diego and buys an M-1 carbine for forty bucks cash. It was probably a souvenir brought back from the war by some Marine or Sea-bee. This guy then goes to L.A. with his new purchase, loads it up and in the middle of the night hides it under that pagoda in front of the house of the guy beating on his sister. He then waits a week or so and organizes an invite to the guy's house. After dark, he goes outside in the back yard to have a smoke, circles around the house to the front and sees the sister beater through the window. He's sitting inside pretty as you please and reading the paper. The guy outside then pulls the carbine out from under the pagoda. He's not worried about fingerprints because he's wearing moleskin gloves. He steadies the weapon on the lattice of the pagoda and fires off nine rounds and kills that brutal bastard just like all those Japs he killed during the war. He throws the gun into the street thinking the cops will figure the shots came from a passing car and that the shooter accidentally dropped the weapon. Then he goes inside and acts all surprised. That's the way it could have happened. But, like I say, it wasn't me who killed Ben. I got witnesses who say I was out in the back yard having a smoke when the shooting started."

"Yeah, I suppose it could have happened like that," I said.

"One thing for sure. That bastard won't be beating on anybody else's sister," said Chick.

"So what about the carbine? Do you want it?" I asked.

"Keep it for a souvenir, or throw it in the ocean. I don't care. It don't belong to me."

There wasn't anything more to be said so I shook Chick's hand, got in my car and headed home. North of Oceanside I turned left onto a dirt road that led to a copse of trees on a bluff over the ocean. I pulled my car behind the trees out of sight from the highway. Seeing no one around, I retrieved the M-1 carbine from my trunk, grasped it by the barrel and flung it as far out in the ocean as I could. The gun floated for a minute or so, the wooden stock fighting a losing battle with the heavier metal parts. Then it sunk out of sight and a succeeding wave washed over the spot.

I got back on US 101 north. I pointed my hood toward home. In my mind, I was planning a new investigation. I was going to track down an airline stewardess named June Chalmers. I was sure that the Western Airlines personnel department would balk at giving me her address or any other information, But hell, I would find it out anyway. After all, Wasn't I a detective?

THE END.

AUTHOR'S NOTE

Thank you for reading my book. If you enjoyed it, won't you please take a moment to leave me a review at your favorite retailer?

Thanks!

D. W. Drake

Sign up for email updates and receive free advance reading copies, updates on new releases, special offers and bonus content. You can contact me directly by email: dwdrake@savanatpress.com

You may also sign up at: www.savanatpress.com

www.ingramcontent.com/pod-product-compliance
Lightning Source LLC
Chambersburg PA
CBHW070742180626
46818CB00007B/2953